Dreaming of a Whyte Wedding

Snow and Bell's Love Story

Written By: A.J. Davidson

CHAPTER 1 SNOW

"What do you mean, she just got snatched?" I yelled behind me as I ran to see what Bell's nephew, Christian, was talking about. By the time I made it outside, all I saw where tail lights turning the corner fast as hell. The sound of tires screeching followed by the engine roaring was heard throughout the neighborhood.

Turning around, I saw Bell running down the stairs, so I ran towards him. Throwing myself into his chest, I sobbed, "Bell, my baby is gone, somebody took my baby. They just went that way!" As I screamed out frantically, I pointed into the direction I saw the car going in. "I think it was blue. No, it was black! Fuck! I don't know which color it was." The look that Bell's face housed was one that even had my soul shook.

"Let's go!" he spat to his brothers as they all jumped into his brother, Prince's SUV. While they were pulling off, I called out to him, "Bell, please find my baby."

"Come on Snow, let's go back inside. They'll find her." Cashmere's hands started pulling at my arm, but I wasn't moving. I refused to go back inside knowing my baby was out there in trouble.

"No, I'm fine right here. I'm not going inside unless my daughter is with me." I said firmly.

"Ok, I'll go inside to call the police. They need to be aware of this even if my brothers do find her."

"What do you mean, if; you think they may not find her? Maybe I should be the one out there looking for her." By the time I turned around to go back inside to get my keys, Sasha was coming outside to tell me the police were on the way. I stood outside impatiently waiting on someone to pull up.

At this moment, it felt like time was standing still.

"All I want is my baby back, I don't care about nothing else at this point. She doesn't deserve no shit like this." I spoke softly as tears dripped from my chin and landed on my shirt. "I don't know who would do something like this or why?"

Soon as I said that, Devin popped in my head. I wanted to give him the benefit of the doubt, but I don't trust that nigga at all, and this sounds like some shit he would do just to fuck with me. "I think I know who probably has her!" I blurted out.

"Tell me who, so we can call my brothers." Sparkle told me as she scrambled through her purse for her phone.

"No fuck them, we can go get her back ourselves. You already know I haven't fucked a nigga up in a minute. My trigger finger is just itching to fuck some shit up." Cash didn't even let me get a word in before she ran back into the house and came back out with her gun. "The fuck y'all standing there looking at me for, get in the damn car and bitch you driving. Toss them heels in the back. I need you to drive this car like you are running from what you been through and you don't want to go back." I dead ass wanted to laugh but now wasn't the time. This bitch is dumb as hell.

Jumping in the car, I pulled off and headed right to Devin's house. I knew he wouldn't be crazy enough to bring her back here, but I was gone wait until that nigga showed up.

"Pass me my phone." I told Sparkle. Grabbing it from her, I called Devin's phone and surprisingly he answered.

"Yea! Who is this?" his voice dragged.

"Bitch don't yea me. Where the fuck is my daughter?" I spat.

"Who the fuck you talking to like that?"

"Nigga, I'm talking to you. You are the only person stupid enough to do some dumb ass shit like this just to get back at me," I told his ass.

"Snow, you better lower your fucking tone and realize who the fuck you are talking to. Don't think 'cause you got with that nigga that I still won't fuck that ass up. Remember who the fuck I am, bitch."

"Yea nigga, and you about to find out who the fuck I am. Now play pussy if you want to, yo ass bout to get fucked tonight and I ain't using no Vaseline." Sparkle and I looked at Cash like she lost all of her mind.

"Oh, you got a lil guard dog now?" he retorted.

"It's Cash bitch, and I'm the wrong bitch to play with. You probably used to beat this bitch ass but you not beating shit over here. Now tell us where Sunshine at, before shit gets real ugly round this bitch. Then yo punk ass really gone find out why they call me, Cashraq!"

"Snow, get this bitch before I do her how I did you. Yo eye healed up yet?" he joked but I didn't find that shit funny at all. "And why the fuck y'all keep asking me about Sunny? You are the one who ran away with her like yo ass could take care of her without me. Now, you tell me where the fuck is my daughter?" he demanded.

"Don't play that innocent role, nigga. Someone snatched her off the street and I know yo trifling ass had something to do with it. I swear Devin if you got my baby, I'm fucking you up and if you don't have her then yo ass know who does." We were around the corner from his house and I was anxious to pull up. This time I wasn't letting him get the best of me. I'm tired of getting my ass whooped. I'm getting my baby and beating his ass the fuck up.

"You better find her by the time I get to you or I'm killing yo new nigga." He told me with his voice laced with venom.

"Ha! We laugh in the face of danger. Ha! Ha! Ha!" Cash taunted. "Bitch suck my brother's dick since you so hard up about him being with Snow. Seems like that's your issue cause you done mentioned his ass twice in a conversation that's supposed to be about your shorty missing." The entire time she was going back and forth with him, I had already parked the car and eased out. "Matter fact keep that same energy. You bitch!"

She ended the call just as Sparkle kicked the front door in. They ran in the house like some niggas while my shit talking ass was watching to see what they were going to do to him first. He was sitting on the couch and didn't have time to even react before they jumped on his ass.

"Bitch if you don't come over here and hit this nigga in the face, I'ma hit you," Cash shouted. Knowing I didn't want that shit, I ran over while they held him down.

"Ouch!" I cried out after hitting him in the face but only hurting myself in the process.

"Snow, my one year old hit harder than that." Sparkle informed me, then nodded her head at Devin. "This is the nigga that you told us used to fuck yo ass up and that's all the anger you have built up in you?"

"No, I have more I just, look, I just want my daughter, that's it and from the looks of things, she's not here."

"I don't give a fuck if she's here or not, getcho fucking lick back." If it wasn't Cash fussing at me, it was Sparkle and they both were right.

"She's not going to do anything because she's weak. Y'all bitches got to the count of one to let me go and get out of my house. Once I stop being nice by letting y'all hold me down, I'm knocking all of you bitches out. Fuck!" he groaned once my foot landed between his legs. Kicking him again, he fell over on his back while holding his dick.

"You raggedy bitch, just wait until I get up."

"You're not getting up!" Cash pulled her gun out and shot him twice; once in both knees. Seeing all of that blood, made me sick to my stomach. "Finish him." She passed me the gun but before I could take it out of her hand, my phone started ringing. I could tell by the ringtone, that it was Bell.

"I gotta get this, it's Bell." I told them before quickly turning away and pressing the phone to my ear.

"I guess yo ass was saved by the Bell. If I was her, I would have killed yo ass and then answered for my nigga." Cash kept talking shit and I tried my best to talk over Devin crying in the background.

"Hey, please tell me you found Sunshine." I blurted out.

"Yea I got her, and you won't believe who took her." he paused for a second as if he were trying to listen to my background. "Who's screaming?"

"Well, I thought Devin had her, so we came over here and -"

"Get y'all ass back over here now. Fuck that nigga, I'll handle his ass later," he spat.

"Cash kind of already did." Biting the inside of my lip, I waited to see what he was about to say.

"Snow, I got Sunshine right here with me. Get my sister back here before she snaps out and end up back in the mental hospital. She will go too far and not know when enough is enough and Sparkle slow ass don't know how to keep her in line."

"Oh shit, I gotta go. We'll be there shortly." Ending the call, I ran over to Cash and pulled the pliers out of her hand. She had them clamped down on his tongue, getting ready to snatch it out of his mouth.

"Let's go Cash, they found my baby." Sparkle and I started pulling her back but her ass was in a zone that no one could pull her out of. "Cash, let's just go make sure my baby is good then I'll bring you back to finish him." I had to say anything to get her to calm down and let go of him.

"You promise?" she asked me.

"I promise. Once I make sure my baby is good, we can come back. Look, you fucked his legs up, where else is he going to go?" Giving in, she walked backwards out the door but kept her eyes trained on Devin, who was still crying and holding his knees. Making it back inside the car, I hauled as back to their mom's house to get to my baby. I looked over at Cash and she was still talking shit and doing gun motions with her hands as if she was shooting someone.

"Don't worry, she'll settle down after she kill his ass. Oh, and don't worry, she's going to remind you to take her back over there." Shaking my head, I pulled up and parked in front of the house.

Running up the stairs, I rushed inside and headed right to the living room. "Sunny!" I called out to her. She turned around and leaped out of her seat; running right towards me. Kneeling down, she wrapped her arms around my neck as tight as she could.

"Mommy, I was so scared. That old lady with no teeth, snatched me up while I was in the middle of learning how to jump Double Dutch. I called out for you, but you weren't there." Just hearing her voice sounding like it she was still frightened, broke me down even more.

"I'm so sorry I wasn't there to protect you. I will never let anything like that happen to you again. I promise you; I will keep you by me at all times." I held her face so that she was looking directly into my eyes as I assured her that I wouldn't let that shit happen again.

"Y'all union real cute and shit, but I thought yo ass was dead." Cringing at the sound of that voice, my eyes widened as I began to search the room to see where it came from. When my eyes landed on her, they involuntarily rolled as we stared at each other in dismay. Of all the fucking people in the world that could have done this shit.

"Mama! You dirty bitch," I blurted out. Walking over to where Bell had her old ass tied up, I took all of the anger that my ass should have had with Devin to smack the fuck out of her.

"Oh, hell no, give me the phone. This fake dead bitch is going to jail for hitting the elderly."

"And yo ass is going to jail for kidnapping, now who do you think they gone keep, you or me?" I questioned.

"Honestly, I hope me because this coota ain't been ate in a minute and I heard they don't give a fuck if gray hair on it or not. They be gay for the stay. I wonder if it's a bitch in there named Butch, so when she has me calling her daddy, it won't sound weird."

"Oh wow!" Bell let out, before grabbing Sunshine's hand and walking out of the room. Turning back to my mama, she sat there with her shoulders slouched and wore an expression on her face as if she didn't give a damn.

"Why would you do something like this?"

"Why not? Someone called me and told me to come and view your body. I knew you were fucking with a nigga with money so that little girl was going to get some insurance money off yo dead ass. I figured if I had her then the money would come to me." She admitted.

"You know it doesn't work like that right? Even if I was dead, she wouldn't be able to touch that money until she was 18. You would have just been taking care of her all of that time with your own money, dummy. How did you know where to find her?"

"Well dummy, if you must know. I had your brother to track the number of the person that called me and told me you were dead. At first, I thought he was the police or something but when I drove up to this neighborhood, I knew he was just a regular ass nigga. I circled the block a few times then I saw my grand baby run outside to play.

Opportunity presented itself, then, Boom! Now I'm here all because I ran out of fucking gas and them niggas saw me. I could have gotten away with it if your brother hadn't forgot to fill my car up like I asked his ass too." I couldn't believe the shit she was saying, and her reason had to be one of the stupidest reasons to kidnap someone.

"All of this, over some money? If you thought your only daughter was dead, why didn't you see if you could get custody of your granddaughter. You never did a damn thing for me, so you could have tried to make up for that with her."

"Chiiiile, who does that? I'm not that grandma that tries to right her rights with the grandchild."

"What?" I asked in confusion, "You mean right your wrongs?"

"No, I meant what the fuck I said. I wasn't wrong for not doing a thing for you, Snow. You were created by a nigga who gave me forty dollars, every time we fucked. Oh, and he would buy me an Italian beef, dipped with cheese and peppers to make sure I was full when I made it home. Nothing was special about you, not even your name. You probably thought it was something sweet and cute behind it, but it wasn't. Have you ever seen snow early in the morning? You know, before people step on it and shit?"

"Yes!" I replied hoping she was about to come with something that wasn't stupid.

"Well your name came about when I was headed to the hospital. The streets were covered in dirty slushy shit, the snow was stepped on and some even had piss on it. Bam, there you have it. You were bound to turn out filthy, dirty, pissy, and stepped on; just like snow."

My vision blurred as I stood there trying to hold in my tears. I began to feel numb all over and the sadder I became, the more my body filled up with rage. Even though I hated the woman that sat before me, I still couldn't bring myself to do anymore harm to her. Yea, I smacked fire from her ass, but if I did more in this moment, I probably would end up killing her.

How could a mother be so fucking evil towards their own flesh? The sad part about this is, I may have my father's color, but I look exactly like this lady. I could never see myself doing anything like this to Sunshine. My heart wasn't set up to be so evil.

"I want so badly to spit on you after I beat cho ass for kidnapping my daughter. But I know that what I want to do isn't nearly as bad as the way God will handle you."

"See, this is where the walked all over part come in at. You never stood up for yourself. You always wanted God to handle some shit. You swear you are miss goodie two shoes and don't have a hateful bone in your body. Get mad bitch! Fight me!" I didn't even feel like going back and forth with her. Kneeling down to get my things, the sound of her hawking up spit caused me to look up right as that bitch spit in my face.

"Don't do it Ms. Celie… she ain't worth it," Cash exclaimed. "That's yo mama, and we only get one of those. You don't need to stoop to her level and cut your blessings off. My mama dead and gone though, so I can beat cho mama ass for you and wouldn't give a fuck. Go in there with your daughter, I'll handle this from here."

"As long as you promise to beat her ass until they won't be able to notice who the fuck she is," I told Cash while I grabbed Sparkle's baby wipes to clean the spit off my face.

"Soo, use the brass knuckles? Cool! I got cha." As I walked out of the room, I began to hear the loud cries of my mother begging Cashmere to stop hitting her. I opened the door to the hall bathroom and stepped inside. Grabbing a towel, I put it in the sink before turning the hot water on.

Taking the hot towel, I laid it on my face then started rubbing my skin off. The more I scrubbed, the more tears would fall. I soon found myself sitting on the toilet seat, crying with my head in my lap.

Defeated wasn't even the right word to describe how I was feeling right now. Today had been one of the worse days of my life and to top it all off, it wasn't even over. Hearing knocks at the door, I softly let them know I was inside and that I'll be out in a minute.

The door knob starting twisting and in walked Bell. Just the sight of him, made me cry even more. Not because I was upset at him, but because I knew my life was so fucked up that I wasn't even worthy of a man like him.

Since the first day we met, it felt like he was pulling me out of this dark ass place. Truth is, I've only been pulling him in the darkness with me. The shit was fucked up and we may as well end this before I cause him anymore turmoil.

CHAPTER 2- BELL

This is not how I expected shit to turn out on Christmas Day. I thought I was going to chill with my family, make memories with my girl and her daughter then get fucked until the date turned to December 26th.

A high-speed chase that quickly turned into a low speed chase, was not in the plan at all. Once Snow told us the direction the car went in, all we had to do was look for the car that was driving like they had a body in the trunk. I'm sure her running out of gas was not a part of her plan, but that worked out perfectly for us.

She talked big shit the whole drive back, until my brother Monte' put his dirty ass sock in her mouth. I didn't know how Snow was going to react knowing it was her mom that did that shit. You got to be one of the sickest parents around to snatch your own grandchild for money.

When their conversation started to go left, I took Sunny to another room and made sure she was good before I left out to check back in on Snow. As I walked down the hallway, I could hear sobbing coming from the bathroom. I knew it couldn't have been neither one of my sisters because they are too tough for tears, so they say, so I knew it was Snow.

Once I pushed the door open, she looked up at me with her face full of tears, then blurted out, "I don't deserve you."

"What? Why would you say something like that?" Pulling her off the toilet lid, I sat down then pulled her back on my lap.

"I'm a mess, my life's a mess, and it's too much for me to handle so I already know you can't," she sobbed.

I chuckled before I knew it, "First off, it ain't shit that I can't handle. You're my girl and I knew about all of your problems before I asked you to be a part of my life. That should have let you know right then, that I didn't give a damn about no shelter, no stupid baby daddy, or no crazy ass mama. I know I'm not your husband but that's my ultimate goal. If a nigga already giving up at the first sign of trouble, then I should be the one saying how I don't deserve you. Look at me," I told her, while cupping her chin.

"You have become so much to me in so little time and I'm not about to let you get away from me that easily. My life is a mess too, I just know how to mask my shit and not allow others to see my troubled side. I'm sure you realized that your friend Sasha, was the same Sasha that I told you about when I was a shorty."

"Yea, I did notice that and I'm sure she's still trying to figure it out, if she hasn't already. She's definitely going to reach out to me so that could be discussed."

"Just seeing her face brought back so many memories of that day. I didn't have a chance to say anything more to her because of the situation with Sunshine and in a way, I'm glad because I didn't know how to explain how I knew her already. What I'm trying to say to you is that, we both have some flaws that we have to deal with. I'm more than willing to help you through yours, while I slowly navigate through my own shit. It may not be peaches and pussy for us all the time, but we gone get through all of this and we gone do that shit together."

"Can we back up a little bit to you saying it may not be peaches and pussy all the time? You know the saying is peaches and cream right?"

"Nah, I don't like cream, but I do like peaches and I love pussy; yours to be exact." Her face turned a blushing red again and the biggest smile stretched across her face.

"What am I going to do with you?"

"Love me long time," I expressed making her laugh. I love the fact that it's the simple shit that I say and do that makes her happy. Not to compare the two, but Yolanda wanted to make a nigga jump through hoops as if she wasn't once where Snow was.

Forgetting the fact that I helped her get out of the shit that she was in. She wasn't humble enough for me, which is why I stopped giving a fuck. She became just live in pussy and that position could have easily been replaced.

"Let's go check on my so called mother before Cash beat her ass to death."

"If you left her alone with Cash, you're about to be planning a funeral." Getting up, we walked out of the bathroom and bumped right into Sparkle. She was running full speed down the hallway.

"Hurry up, I think Cash made your mom have a heart attack. While Cash was beating her ass, she fell over and started holding her chest." Snow stopped walking and instead of going to check on her mom, she started walking in the opposite direction. Hustling behind her, I pulled her back towards me.

"What's wrong shorty? You're not going to check to make sure she's good?"

"You're kidding right? That lady just said some mean ass shit to me, and you think I give a fuck if the Devil is calling her ass home? Hell no! On top of her saying I was a worthless piece of shit, she tried to kidnap my daughter. That's not even a person I would piss on if she was on fire." I knew she was pissed off, but at the end of the day, that was still her mother.

"Regardless of how a person does you, don't fuck up the good shit that you have going on just to meet them on their level. My mama and I didn't always see eye to eye, nor did she always agree with the road I picked to go down. One thing about it, she still knew she could count on me for anything and I knew I could for her too. I was the first one out of all of my sisters and brothers to do anything for her.

My mama gone, Snow bunny, and I can't get that time back with her. Yo mama still here and even if she decides to not fuck with you after you've helped her, then that's between her and God," I paused for a second and thought over that part, "Or whoever she's going to see in the afterlife," I finished."

I tried to tell her everything that I knew in my heart that was right to do. Everybody don't get that chance to make shit right with their parents. "Trust me when I say, I'm all for you saying fuck yo mama her, but after you make sure her ass is not dying in my mama house. Also, you'll never know how being good to her, even after she's been mean to you, could actually change her evil ass heart."

"Ugh! She not like dead... dead, but she will be if we don't get her to the hospital." Sparkle interrupted as she poked her head into the room. I guess all of that talking helped because even though Snow, didn't say anything she still got up and walked out of the room with my sister. Sparkle called the ambulance, while Cash sat back and rolled a blunt like she wasn't the cause of shit.

"Say Snow, why you ain't tell me yo mama heart wasn't strong? I would've beat her ass with just my fist and not the brass knuckles if I had known her heart was weak like that," Cash said casually.

"Cash, I haven't seen my mama in years. I wouldn't have known had a heart by the way she used to treat me."

"Then why we saving her? Let her ass gone on down to the lower room and Rest in Piss." Shaking my head at Cash, as I picked her mama up from the floor. She wasn't saying anything to either of us, but her face looked like she was in a lot of pain. Hearing the ambulance pull up, they rushed inside and checked her vital signs. One of the EMT's was my classmate in high school and that's the one who stood up and pulled me to the side.

"Everything seems to be fine; her blood pressure is actually excellent for someone that's claiming to be having a heart attack. We will take her in anyway just to do more test but I think-"

"She's faking?" I said, finishing his sentence. I looked over at her on the couch and she was already looking at me through one eye and the other one was closed.

"I can't say those exact words and make it seem like I'm disregarding what everyone is saying is wrong with her but it's definitely not a heart attack." He started to walk away but quickly turned back around towards me. "Oh, and who's going to explain the way her face look when we get to the hospital. Is she in some type of domestic violence relationship?"

"Nah this shit right here is pure family violence. If they want to know the truth about what led up to her getting her ass whooped, then I'm sure everyone in here would be more than happy to tell their side," I told him.

"Cool, just have that story together by the time we make it, then y'all good." After letting him know that we will be fine, I followed them out of the door but stopped walking when I saw Sasha sitting on the steps with her kids. I wasn't ready for this conversation, but I guess I've put it off long enough.

"Hey, it's Bell, right?" She asked as she stood up from the steps and walked over to me. Snow came outside with her purse in one hand and Sunshine in the other. She looked like a deer caught in the headlights as she looked between the two of us.

"Sasha, what are you doing back here? I thought you were gone." Snow spoke to her, as I stood back in the doorway.

"Yea well, by the time we made it back, it was after 8 and you already know Cruella wasn't letting us in. I also needed to talk to your guy for a second, if you don't mind." *Shit, I mind.*

"No, I don't mind. How about you take the girls inside and I'll leave Sunshine here with Sparkle. You can ride to the hospital with us and you guys can just talk there," Snow told her.

"Y'all must think this is the baby sitters club or something. I'm going to the hospital too. I need to make sure that heffa doesn't say my damn name when they start asking her who fucked her ass up like that." Cash came outside fussing and cleaning her brass knuckles off.

"I'll watch them all, bring' em inside." Sparkle ushered all of the kids inside, then closed the door. I allowed all of them to walk ahead of me while I took this time to gather my fucking thoughts.

"Bell, I'll drive my car because I got a B.C. after this." Cash told me, as she walked away.

"What's a B.C?"

"A booty call," she explained.

"Yo ass!" I chucked, "Aight, I'll see you at the hospital."

"Oh, after we make sure her mama good, I do need you to roll back over to her ex dude house with me. Hopefully that muthafucka bleed to death or something but he doesn't need to live to see tomorrow."

"Bet!" Was all I said as I got inside of the car. Snow and Sasha were already inside. As I pulled off, the car was silent as hell; a little too silent for me.

When we pulled up to the hospital, Snow stepped out of the car with no sense of urgency. You could tell that she was only going to check on her because I told her it was the right thing to do. If it were up to her, she would have been in Christmas pajamas laid across my lap, watching *The Color Purple.*

"Bell!" She dragged and threw her arms around my waist. As she looked up at me, I looked down at her and then kissed her forehead. "Are you sure I have to go inside? Can't they just check her out then take her to jail for kidnapping my daughter?"

"No, they can't, and yes you need to go inside. I know she fucked up but just be the bigger person just this one time. Make sure she's good and send her on her way. You only get one mama-" Before I could say anything else, Sasha cleared her throat. I swallowed the lump in mine, before continuing. "Go inside just to make sure she's good and by the time you come back out I should be done talking with Sasha, ok?"

"Ok, you sure you don't need me out here?" I laughed at how she poked her lip out, trying to look sad.

"Nah, I need you to go inside." Folding her arms up, she stomped off and headed inside the hospital. I tried to watch her walk away as long as I could to hold off the inevitable. This conversation needed to be had years ago and should be easier to talk about now but for some reason, I don't think this shit about to go well at all. Not knowing if I should start off with, I'm sorry, or just reach out and hug her until she has released all of her anger that she had towards me right now.

"The day of my mother's funeral, someone gave me an envelope full of money, then walked away quickly. I only caught a glimpse of his face but the more I look at you now, I see his face. Was that you?" I was happy that she started the conversation but I didn't expect her to go that far back in the past.

"It was," I admitted.

"Then I saw you again at school. You beat this guy up for talking about my clothes."

"Yes, that was me too," I replied honestly.

"Why?" she asked. I could see the tears building up before I said anything. What she asked was a good question but for some reason, I felt like it was unnecessary. Why would the why matter as long as I made sure she was good until she just up'd and moved away?

"I felt like I owed that to you. What happened to your mom was an accident but-"

"But because of that accident, I had to live my life without my mama. If you and your brothers had not fucked with any of us from the beginning, then she wouldn't have chased you across the street. I mean, yea, she could have looked before running across the street then she would have seen the bus but still; this falls on you guys. She was all I had, and my dad was living on the streets too, so I couldn't go stay with him. It would have been me going from boxes to a tent but still I couldn't depend on him.

Instead, the system sent me to go live with my auntie, and that wasn't any better. My uncle, her husband, used to fuck the shit out of me and once she found out that he knocked me up, I had to go. Life has not been easy for us and I honestly feel like, all of that was only a domino effect."

"So, your daughters?" I questioned.

"Are his!" *Damn!* She broke down crying and that made me feel even worse.

"Look, I know I can't bring your mom back, and I know money can't fix it either, but I can help you. We can start by getting you guys out of the shelter. I can give you a house, a condo or an apartment; whichever you want. I'll even pay all of the utilities for two years. That will give you enough time to get on your feet." I felt good after letting all of that out. I have the means to help, I just hope she accepts it.

"I don't want your money, I won't my mom back. Can your money bring her back?" She bucked up and as I tried to console her, she started swinging on me. I didn't stop her because I deserved every last one of those licks. I let her hit me until she was tired and the only thing she could do was fall into my arms and cry.

"Please, just let me help you. I can write a check right now for 150,000 thousand dollars. If your mom would have had life insurance, that would have been around the amount you would have received. I know there's no price on losing a loved one, but shit, I'm standing here offering you up everything including my fucking soul right now. I even have a car for you too. You have no idea how hard I looked for you when you moved away. After your mom passed, I tried to stay as close to you as possible so I could be there for you even without you knowing I was there.

I'm not a fucked up person, I just made a few bad decisions in my life and I'm standing here bearing it all right now. Just allow me to help you get to where you need to or should have been in life. Please!" I poured it all out to her and I couldn't even be upset if she turned it all down because that wasn't enough for her. There's nothing I could do or say to change any of this, but I swear, I'ma try until she just flat out tells my ass to leave her the fuck alone.

"Money won't change anything. I'll still be this uneducated black bitch with kids by her auntie's husband."

"Man Sasha, stop that shit. Yea, you were dealt a bad hand, but we can shuffle this shit back in the deck and get five more cards and win this shit. Just trust me, I promise, just like I got Snow, I got you too."

"I don't know Bell. I don't think I can be pulled out of the shit I'm in. It's rough." She let out with a sigh.

"Let me make it easy," I replied quickly. After talking a little while longer, she finally agreed to accepting my help. I called my driver to come pick her up to take her back to my mom's house to get her kids.

Tonight, she's going to stay at my hotel and then

tomorrow we will pick her up and let her decide on

which place she wants to live in. I just pray that her

accepting my help is something that she really does want

to do and this shit won't come back and bite me in the

ass later.

As they drove off, I headed inside to find Snow.

Giving her a call, she answered and told me what floor

her mom was on. The tone of her voice told me that

something was wrong, and she only confirmed the

feeling by telling my ass to hurry the fuck up.

I walked in to the room as all hell was about to

breaking loose. "Whoa...whoa... whoa! Snow stop!" I

shouted and pulled her back from the cord the was

connected to her mom's I.V. She had it around her throat

and was trying to strangle the fuck out of her mom.

"What the fuck is wrong with you? Yo ass trying to go to jail?" I asked Snow as I held her from the back.

"You better get her before I give her ass the whooping she should have gotten as a kid," her mom blurted out breathlessly.

"They are saying she has to be released into my care and I don't want this bitch at my house. I figured if her ass was dead then she wouldn't even make it out of the hospital," Snow admitted.

"And you wouldn't make it back home to see your daughter if they would have caught you. Now, calm yo ass down. What did they say was wrong with her?"

"Crazy, she faked her damn heart attack. It was only gas but because she keeps saying that she's in pain, they just want me to keep a close eye on her at home."

"Why can't she just stay here, and they observe her?" I asked.

"The dummy doesn't have any insurance and they need the bed."

"Then do what you have to do to get her straight so she could go back to where she came from. You did what I asked you to do and that's all that matters to me. Once they clear her, I'll send her on the first thing smoking back to Romeoville."

"What y'all not gone do is talk about me like I ain't laying here. I don't want to stay with her, just like she doesn't want me to. I don't trust neither one of you anyway. Especially not that fucking-"

"What's up Cashmere," I spoke as she walked into the room. "Snow's mom was just talking about you. What were you about to say about her?"

"I was about to say how pretty she was and that she sure knows how to throw a left hook." She smiled through the bruises.

"I'm glad you feel that way. I thought I was going to have to kill yo ass if you told these people I beat cho ass."

"Oh no no no no! I would never do such a thing like that. You have my word, Ms. perfect brass knuckle slinger." I think Cash scared the shit out of this old lady 'cause she was just about to talk mad shit about her.

"Yea, better not. Anyway, are you ready to go holla at this nigga Devin? We gotta make sure that nigga act like Snow's mama if someone finds his ass alive." Once I made she sure Snow and her mama were good, Cash and I left out of the room. We had to quickly move out of the way because they were pushing an irate patient pass and into the room next door.

"I swear to y'all, I'm killing that bitch. She shot me in both knees like I was a weak bitch. Do y'all know who the fuck I am? I'm Devin the fucking dude, you hear me. I'm that fucking nigga," he yelled out as they positioned the bed to push it inside of the room.

"Please get him a sedative!" The doctor called out and told one of the nurses. Cash and I looked at each other before slowly dipping back inside the room.

"This shit just got a little more interesting. Now I don't have to go to his crib. I just gotta knock out a nurse, put on her uniform, then go into his room and kill his ass. Boom, five minutes later, I'm slipping back out of his room and out of those clothes," Cash explained.

"Let me know how much yo bond is." I told her as she left out of the room without even allowing me to tell her ass that was a dumb ass idea.

Turning back towards Snow, it was like she and her mom were having a stare off. They both hated each other in the worst way, and it was written on both of their faces.

Chapter 3 Sasha Barrett

As I road in the backseat of this nice ass SUV, I couldn't help but to continue to shed tears over my mother. I don't even know if taking things from him was the right idea, but he wasn't going to take no for an answer. I hated to even give him the impression that things were cool now because they weren't. I still have the same hate in my heart for him, that I did the day my mom died in my arms.

We were already down bad and having some bad ass little boys come through and snatch the only money you had left to feed your child was a horrible feeling. She chased them more so to scare the shit out of them because she knew she really wasn't catching they ass. Everything happened so fast and even if I did yell out to her that a bus was coming, it still would have been too late.

I miss my mama so much and even though we were on the streets, she still tried to stay positive. She would always tell me that nothing last forever and we won't be like this much longer. I prayed every day that we woke up to our forever finally ending. Going to school was rough because I smelled like the environment, I lived in.

Teachers would try to help, but mama would only curse them out and let them know that she's doing the best that she could. I know one thing, they couldn't say she was unfit even on her worse day because I was always provided a shelter. Regardless if we were in a tent, a box, or a shelter; I had somewhere to sleep.

My stomach was full, because she was either going to take someone's last bite or create some shit. At one point we had everything but once she lost her job, it seemed like everything started hitting her at once. She did her best and I could never fault her for that part.

The only people I fault, were Bell and his stupid ass brothers. The hope I had of survival left when the main person that taught me how to survive, left me alone. Years and years rolled by, and I never caught that break she promised me would come. Forever lasted longer than she mentioned too.

When they finally caught up with my auntie, her only concern was if the state were going to pay her for taking me in. She didn't give a fuck about me. I ate more with my mama on the streets, than I did with a bitch that had a full fucking kitchen.

My uncle was like my savior, whenever she would get angry and try to beat my ass, he would stop her. I thought he was really trying to protect me, turns out that was only his way of getting closer to my coochie. I was 14 years old when he first started fucking me like I was a grown ass woman. Crying and asking him to stop, only made him do it harder while kissing my tears away. The shit was fucked up and became even more fucked up when I had my daughter Nevaeh at fifteen years old.

I couldn't tell my auntie that my daughter was her husband's child, so I lied and told her I was raped by some guys at school. She didn't dig deep so, I thought everything was cool. Until the 2nd baby rolled around at the age of eighteen. By then, I didn't give a fuck what she knew about her husband, it's not like I asked for the shit. I learned about child support and food stamps through the welfare office and I needed those coins. I had paperwork mailed to him requesting that he went to the office for a DNA test. I fucked up by still living in the house with them at the time. Once she saw my name on the paper, she came right into the room and tried to whoop my ass. That only led to her ass getting beat the fuck up and our asses out on the streets.

We left her house and moved to the projects. We were good there, until this nigga I started dating tricked me into move with him. He was a dog ass nigga, but I stayed because living with him, was better than staying in a shelter with my girls. So, for years I stayed quiet regardless of how many bitches he would sleep with or how many would come to me as a woman. I eventually got tired of that shit and told him he needed to respect me or it was over. Before I got the words out of my mouth all the way, he had our asses out his house. Shit, I even thought about putting them up for adoption, but they were too damn big. At that time, Nevaeh was nine and Angel was six. They would have been in the system forever, so I just chose to do what I had to do. Every day I told them the same shit my mama told me, forever doesn't last always and we won't be like this much longer.

The truck came to a stop and snapped me out of my thoughts. When the driver opened the door, I stepped out and shook from wind that was blowing hard as hell. He was grinning from ear to ear, as if he saw something he liked. I was confused because I was standing here looking like a whole dust rag. Nodding my head, I walked right on by him and headed inside of the house.

"Nevaeh and Angel, it's time to go!" I called out to them. Sunshine came running in first, followed by Sparkle with the girl's coats and hats.

"Girl, I'm so glad you're back. Get these bad ass kids."

"I'm sorry. They knew to be on their best behavior."

"It wasn't just them, all of these kids lost their home training," I laughed as I closed the front door behind me. "They are some really sweet kids," she stated, as she smiled down at them.

"Thank you." Putting on their coats, we stepped outside into the night air.

"Mommy, who's truck is that?" Angel asked.

"It's Mr. Bell's, so get in and let's go see the nice surprise that he has for us." They both started cheering, before jumping inside of the truck. I couldn't wait for them to see where we were staying tonight. Shoot, I couldn't even wait to see where we were staying tonight.

"Do you ladies need anything to eat before we arrive at the hotel?" The driver asked us.

"No, I don't have money," I admitted.

"I didn't ask you if you had money? I asked if you wanted to eat." He spoke in a tone that put me at ease. How? I don't know but it was something about his voice that calmed my spirit.

"Well girls, what do want?" I asked them.

"Anywhere you want!" he added.

"My friends at school would always talk about this place called Chuck E' Cheese." Navaeh let out in a squeal.

"No baby, he didn't mean a place like that. Plus, it's not open this late. Matter fact, there isn't much open tonight, it's Christmas." I reminded them..

"Good thing I know the owner. Let's go girls!" He had them all excited and they both yelled out "Yay!" Shaking my head, I laughed at the excitement that poured out of them.

"I'm sorry, I don't remember getting your name," I stated.

"I'm Timothy, but you can just call me Tim," he replied while looking in the mirror at me. "And you are?"

"Sasha."

"And I'm Navaeh and I'm ten. This is my little sister Angel and she's seven. She think she's the oldest just because her birthday is in February and mine is in June."

He laughed before replying back to her, "Nice to meet you Navaeh and Angel. I hope you guys enjoy yourself here because we have the place all to ourselves. I'll even throw us a few pizza's in the oven," He announced, making my stomach growl.

"Oh my gosh mommy, I haven't had pizza in soooo long." Angel blurted out.

"Well tonight you are going to get unlimited pizza and soda until you pass out. Then after that, we will swing by this nice little toy store I just opened up and you can grab as many dolls as your little arms can carry."

"Nooo," I dragged, "they do not need all of that." I had to step in because I didn't need them thinking this was something they would be getting on the regular. I'm barely keeping my head above water as it is.

"Yesss," he dragged trying to match my tone, "just let them enjoy themselves for the moment. It's not everyday kids are lucky enough to just run through a store and grab anything they want; take advantage. Plus, it's less stuff you will have to buy later."

"But what if I can't keep this happiness going for them? I don't need them looking at me as if I took this away from them."

"Then I'll work everything out for you." When he assured me that everything would be ok, that calming feeling came over me again. "Now girls, are you ready to have some fun?" he squealed just as loud as they did, making them laugh at him.

Opening the door to the truck, they leaped out and raced him to the door. I was happy for them but confused at the same time. I wanted to ask him why was he being so nice to us but I didn't want to seem ungrateful. By the time I made it inside, he was washing their hands and placing them on the counter top. Grabbing a towel, I dried their hands off and stood beside them so they wouldn't fall.

"Can I have pickles on my pizza?" Angel asked.

"Eww! That's nasty, sister." Navaeh gave Angel the stank face, real quick. "I want pineapples on my pizza instead of pickles."

"What are you supposed to say girls?" I asked them.

"Now!" Navaeh spat.

"No, you're supposed to say please." Angel corrected.

"Girl bye," Navaeh came back with. These two were going to give me a run for my life. I couldn't say money because I didn't have much of that shit.

"How about we do half and half. Then I'll make a separate pizza for mommy and me." Tim suggested. They made a mess of the kitchen before running off to play. While the pizza's cooked, Tim and I cleaned up the kitchen.

"You know you didn't have to do any of this, right?" I asked him.

"I know, but I wanted to do it."

"Ok, but why?" I had to ask.

"Because I'm a good guy and I like helping people and doing things to put a smile on their faces. That's a joy I only wished I could get back as a kid."

"Well, I definitely don't wish to go back to my childhood. It's wasn't very pretty," I admitted.

"But you can make your future outshine all of that shit. My life wasn't the best, but we made the best of this shit. This driver shit ain't the only thing I do. I just do it cause the nigga break good bread with me. I own a toy store, sell bundles, clothes, and shoes. Shit, I'm a walking outlet mall, shorty." I laughed so hard at that.

"I need some clothes. You see me looking like raggedy ann?"

"Regardless of that, you still have a smile on your face and that showed a side of you that I would love to get to know. Those clothes didn't scare me. It's bitches;

excuse me, women! My bad!" He corrected once he saw my brows snap together. "I've met women who have everything designer under the sun, and they are some of the dirtiest muthafuckas.

I can tell that you are different, just by the way you didn't bat one eyelash at me when you got out the truck earlier. Most women, would have seen the expensive suit, the truck and thought; oh this nigga got money. Sure enough, they would have walked away just like you did. But, they would have been throwing that ass so hard to get my attention that they damn near break their backs." He mocked the way that they walked, making me laugh. "I do want to get to know you though. That's only if you allow me to." I was shocked as hell when he let those words slip out of his mouth.

"You're kidding right?" I spat. "You do know we were just homeless like two seconds ago, right?"

"But you're not now, so what's the problem?"

"I have nothing to offer you. Literally, I have nothing at all." I admitted to him. I barely have a pot to piss in, and I definitely do not have a window to throw it out of."

"But you will, and until you have more to give me, just allow me to pour all that I have out to you. I ain't asking for your hand in marriage, I'm just asking to be your friend so that I could get to know you better." Looking him over, my eyes scanned his entire structure and was pleased. Tim was definitely sexy as hell, but I had no clue what the hell he saw in me.

"We will just have to see about that. Bell is supposed to be giving me somewhere to live, so once I get us settled and my life back to normal, then I'll see what I can do. Until then, I just need to focus on getting back on the right track."

"Let me change your mind." He stated, while stepping closer to me. His minty voice sent a chill down my spine and caused me to quiver. Tim stood a strong 6'3, light skin, with light brown eyes. The little gap in between his teeth was even sexy. I could tell by the way his suit clung to him, that his body was sexy as hell underneath.

I couldn't believe that someone like he, really wanted to get to know someone like me. Here I was standing here in some clothes that had been handed down so many times, they were faded. Mr. Jordan always dropped boxes of clothes that he bought from the Goodwill off at the shelter. I always tried to catch him as soon as he walked in, so I could get my hands on the descent stuff for my girls and I.

"Sooo, you gone turn me down, but stare at me like I'm a piece of meat?"

"What? I was not looking at you like that. I was just in a daydream, my bad."

"Yea, a dream that had your ass biting the bottom of your lip while staring at my dick print." I was so embarrassed, but he obviously wasn't. He grabbed his dick and my face really started blushing. "I don't know what type of man you think I am, Ms. Sasha, but I don't get down like that on the first night. You gotta take me out before you get a piece of this good dick." I laughed out so loud that I had to quickly cover my mouth.

"Oh my gosh! I was not looking at your meat. I mean, it is visible, but I wasn't staring at it. Like I said, I was just daydreaming."

"Yea, about this dick," he barked, making me feel so embarrassed.

"What's that smell?" Nevaeh came into the kitchen and asked.

"Oh shit!" Tim rushed over to the oven and pulled the pizza's out. "You girls like cajun?" They both looked at each other before Angel replied to him.

"We've had worse. Grab the pizza cutter and let's eat." He tried his best to make the pizza presentable but that didn't work. They were so burnt that we ended up eating salads until we were stuffed. Once we finished here, we left and went to the toy store as he promised them. They loaded up on everything they knew I couldn't afford.

"You sure you got enough?" he asked them.

"Yes sir," Nevaeh replied, "Mom told us not to be greedy before we walked inside." Her ass threw me all under the bus.

"And I told your mom not to worry about it because everything was on the house. Now, go put that stuff in a basket and get whatever else you can fit inside."

"Yay!" Angel shouted, "We like him mommy. He's nice like uncle Ronnie used to be to us. You know, before Auntie Daisy kicked us out the house."

"Girls, go get whatever else you need so we can get to the room and get you guys into bed," I let out quickly.

"Yes, ma'am." They replied in unison before running off. I didn't want to look at Tim after she said that, because I knew he was going to ask questions.

"You can go get a toy too," he told me.

"What am I going to do with a toy?" I replied.

"Shit! Take the edge off," he shrugged his shoulders before easing down the aisle. "I'm sure one of these muthafuckas vibrate. I know for sure, I got a tickle me Elmo back there. That muthafucka shake like an old school Cadillac."

"You don't care what you say," I told him as we laughed then walked off to find the girls. He let us get in the truck while he stayed back a moment. Ten minutes later, he came out with a gift bag and a big smile. After putting everything in the truck, we headed to the hotel. Once we arrived, he ran inside to get the keys.

"Did you girls have fun?" I asked

"Yes, ma'am." They replied as the truck door came open.

"I got the room keys, are you ready?" he asked. Nodding our heads, we got out the truck and waited on him to grab somethings out the truck. "I'm sure I will have to pick you up tomorrow so you can just take a toy a piece inside for now," he told them before turning to me, "Oh, this is for you." He passed me the bag that he walked out of the toy store with.

"Do I want to ask what this is?"

"Nope, now let's go," he retorted. The girls and I, were in awe of how nice the hotel looked. When we made it to the room, our eyes really got bucked.

"Wow! This is nice mommy," Angel let out.

"I know right," I agreed.

"Take this in the room while I talk to mommy for a second."

"Yes sir." They ran off and left us alone. He then passed me another bag from walmart. "Snow, left this at the front desk. I guess we took longer than expected to get here so she told them that these things were for you and the girls."

"Thanks." Taking the bag, I sat it down on the table before turning back to him.

"Don't open that gift I gave you until the girls are asleep and you have gotten out the shower. Once you open it up, I want you to call me and thank me," he grinned.

"Thank you for what?"

"For taking the edge off." He gave me this sneaky ass smile while handing me his business card. "Use that whenever you feel like it, aight?"

"I will." Taking the card out of his hand, I looked down and read the front of it. "Timothy Whyte!" I blurted out, "You're Bell's brother?"

"Ugh yes. You didn't know that?"

"You killed my mother!" I spat, catching him off guard.

"Nawl, G! I've never kill anybody in my life. I mean, I ran over a squirrel once, but that was it. I even felt bad about that shit by the time I got home."

"Get out!" I shouted, with tears in my eyes as I pushed him out the door.

"Wait Sasha, who is your mother?" Not replying to him, I slammed the door in his face. Placing my back against the door, I slid down to the floor. Pulling my knees to my chest, I started crying even harder. I knew he had to know who I was. If Bell knew then he should have known too. Why would he try to get to know me knowing that it would only end up like this? Using my shirt, I cleaned my face then blew my nose. I was so irritated and pissed off that I got up from the floor and stormed over to the gift he bought me. Picking it up, I threw it against the wall.

"What the hell?" I blurted out when the box started vibrating fast as hell. I opened it, only to see a tickle me Elmo inside with a note attached that read. *Just to take the edge off.*

CHAPTER 4- TIMOTHY WHYTE

I stood outside of the room door looking lost as fuck. I wasn't sure of what just happened because the shit happened so fucking fast. "Pulling out my phone, I called up my brother as I walked away from the door.

"What's good? They straight?" He asked right as he picked up the phone.

"Yea they are good, but I'm not. Sasha and I been kicking it with the girls since we left the hospital. I got ready to head home, so I gave her my business card. She sees my name on the card and flip the fuck out. It was like shorty had that fifteen crazy bitches' syndrome or some shit like that. She started saying how I killed her mama. I instantly stopped her like, hell nah my guy; I haven't killed anyone but Sandy."

"Sandy?" He interrupted.

"Yea, a fucking squirrel. What in the hell is she even talking about, bruh?" That long ass pause he gave me is what had my ass worried for real. Had a nigga trying to think back far as fuck to see if I've ever killed an old bitch before.

"You remember when we were kids and we were fucking with them homeless muthafuckas? It was a lady with a little girl who started chasing us one day after we took her money out her hand." I stood at the elevator door and thought back to that day.

"Yep, and her old ass got hit by that bus, right?"

"That little girl was her and-"

"That was her fucking mama!" I finished. Ain't this about a bitch!" Running my hands down my face, as I tried to think of a way to fix this shit. "I'll hit you back later on, I'm bout to go back and holla at her." Ending the call, I headed back to the room. I must've knocked

about twenty times before Nevaeh answered the door.

"My mommy is in the shower."

"Ok, do you mind if I wait inside for her?" I

asked.

"Only if you go get that black Barbie out the

truck for me. I forgot her and that's the one I really

wanted to play with tonight."

"I got you. I'll be right back." I went to the truck

and got pissed because all of the fucking dolls were

black barbies. I didn't know which one she was talking

about. Grabbing a handful, I hustled back to the room.

When I made it back inside of the room, Sasha was still

in the shower. I laid on the floor and played Barbie with

the girls until I heard crying coming from the bathroom.

"I'll be right back. Let me go check on mommy."
Getting up from the floor, I knocked on the bathroom door gently but she didn't answer me. Walking in, I saw her sitting under the shower water with her hands covering up her face. Taking my shoes and socks off, I grabbed a towel before pulling the shower doors back. Turning the water off, I wrapped the towel around her to cover up her body. She looked up at me and started crying even more. That shit broke my heart.

Stepping inside, I sat down behind her and held her tight. All I got out of my mouth was, "I'm sorry," before she started crying so hard that it sounded like she was hyperventilating. "I swear, I didn't mean for any of that to happen. We were just kids and didn't know she would react like that. If I could take that day back, I swear I would. Just tell me what you want me to do to make things right. I don't want you to push me away because of this."

"What else am I supposed to do? When I see you now, all I'm going to do is think about that day." she cried out.

"We just have to find other ways to help you cope. I'll pay for whatever it is because I don't want you holding this in. Just allow me to help you. Please." Shaking her head, no, she pushed me off her before standing to her feet. The towel slipped off her and she just stood there with a face full of tears. I should have gotten right up and out of the shower but a nigga dick got hard as fuck by looking at her body.

For shorty to be homeless, her body was still nice as hell. She ain't missed as many meals as she claims she have. Getting up, I pulled her close to me then wrapped my arms around her.

Kissing her once on the forehead, I whispered, "I'm sorry." I tried to lift her head up so that she was looking at me, but she kept her eyes closed.

"Look at me," I said sternly, "I'm dead ass sorry shorty." I stood there and looked into her eyes. Her skin was the color of dark roasted coffee. The short hair she rocked was flat earlier but since she sat under the water, now her little curls were all over her head. Shorty, was thicker than cold grits and even in her most vulnerable stage, she was still beautiful as hell.

I found myself kissing her on her lips over and over. At first, she wouldn't kiss me back and I didn't expect her to. But, when she did, my dick reacted to her soft touch and stood at attention. She wrapped her arms around my neck and some kind of way, my slacks were down to my knees and my dick was out.

Lifting herself up, she wrapped her legs around my waist. I should have protected myself but it was too late now because I was already inside. As I entered her fully, she gripped me tighter as if she was bracing herself for the dick that was about to be all up in her guts.

Turning around, I pressed her back against the wall, while I slowly slid in and out of her. Her moans were sending me to another level. As she bit into my shoulder, she started trying to match my thrust. I'm usually the one in control, but she was trying to take over.

Placing my hands under her ass cheeks, I lifted her up so I could regain control. Slamming her down on my dick, I went deeper inside of her; making her moan louder. "Shh, the girls might hear you." Nodding her head, she tried to cover her mouth but that didn't work.

"Fuck!" I hissed as she bit into my neck to muffle her moans. Lifting her off me, I turned her around, rubbed my fingers up and down her slit before sliding back inside. Her pussy was so warm and gushy. You could tell that ain't nobody touched that shit in a minute.

Gripping her waist, I slid in and out of her tight ass walls. She would grip my dick with her pussy and it felt like she was pulling the nut out of me.

"Fuck, I'm about to cum," she growled. I started beating her shit up even faster until I felt I was about to cum too.

Pulling out, I let my kids ride the back of their future mama as I nutted on her back. She stood up, then turned the shower water back on.

"You can go now." she told me in a nonchalant tone while washing her body.

"Damn, a nigga can't wash his dick off?" I asked her. She didn't say a word, just kept washing her ass. Picking up my wet ass clothes, I stepped out the shower. I started drying off but that shit was pointless if I was about to put back on some wet ass clothes.

Seeing her Walmart bag on the counter, I went through it while she wasn't looking. Grabbing me a gown and some leggings, I threw them on. As soon as I bent down to put my shoes on, I bust right out of them. When I opened the bathroom door, the girls looked at me and started laughing.

"You look like a mommy." Angel blurted out followed by loud giggles from them both.

"Yea, well blame yo mama for this. Goodnight girls."

"Goodnight Mr. Tim." they said in unison.

I tried to get out of there as fast as I could without anyone seeing my ass in this girly shit. It was cold as fuck outside so I'd rather have this on, instead of some wet clothes. Jumping in my truck, I pulled my phone out then sent a text to my brother.

Me: GTD

Hitting send, I laughed at the meaning behind those letters. When I heard Martin and Tommy say that shit, I was rolling loud as hell.

Lil Bruh: Yo ass going to hell for that shit dawg. Leave her alone if yo intentions aren't good bruh. For real.

Me: Boy fuck you. My intentions are as good as this, I'm sorry dick I just gave her ass.

Lil Bruh: Aight G. That's on y'all. Be easy. We are leaving mama house.

Me: Bet. Call me in the morning to let me know where to bring them.

Tossing the phone to the side, I pulled off and headed home. A nigga was tired as hell. I went right inside and took me a good shower before getting in the bed. I felt like a shorty who just got a new pair of J's and was anxious as shit to wear them bitches to school tomorrow. I was hoping she called me before she went to sleep but that didn't happen. After a while, I finally fell asleep.

CHAPTER 5 SNOW

"It's your sister." Groaning, I rolled over towards Bell with my phone in my hand. "Hello," I whispered in a groggy tone.

"The deal is done and it's a dead deal." Pulling the phone from my ear, I handed it right to Bell.

"Yea!" he bellowed into the phone. "What?" he paused to let her speak. "How?" Pausing again, but this time I sat up because I was anxious to know what all of that was about. "Aight, good looking out." Ending the call, he pulled me to him then kissed me on my forehead.

"What was all of that about?" I quizzed.

"Oh, she killed Devin." He let out without an ounce of give a fuck in his voice. I didn't know if I were supposed to be happy or sad. I know I'm supposed to hate him for all of the shit that he has done to me, but I can't lie like I don't feel a way right now.

"If you cry, I'm fucking the shit out of you until you are happy again." When he said that, I made myself cry. I wasn't crying at first, but a bitch was horny and needed to get fucked in the worst way. After the shit we went through yesterday with Sunny and later with my mom at the hospital, I needed me some good dick.

"Cool, dick it is." Flipping on top of me. He tore my panties off then fucked the shit out of me like he said he would. Twenty minutes later, jumping in the shower to get our day started. He told me about the conversation that he had with Sasha and I was happy that she took his offer to help her. She could be how I used to be at times and rather reject help. Just to struggle to make a way out of no way so no one would be able to say that they did something for me.

"Ay, don't say nothing aight?"

"Boy, what is it? Who else do I talk to besides yo ass anyway?" I asked him.

"Tim fucked Sasha." My neck snapped around quick as fuck.

"Stop yo shit. I don't even believe that. Sasha had the girls with her, and she doesn't seem like the type that would just I give it up for a ride home."

"Well, she gave it up for some reason. All I know is the nigga text me and said G.T.D." I started looking puzzled as hell because I had no idea what those letters stood for. Bell must have known I was lost as hell because he started laughing and shaking his head. "It meant he, got the draws. He got that shit from an episode of Martin when he was talking to Tommy."

"Remind me to smack his crazy ass for that shit. He could have kept that to himself." Shaking my head, I threw on a Fila sweat suit and some shoes to match before heading down the hallway to wake up Sunny.

"Sunny, it's time to wake up!" I called out to her. Pulling the covers back, I started panicking when I saw her bed was lined with pillows. Leaving out of her room, I ran back down the hallway and into my room. "I think my mama took Sunny. She's not in her room."

"She not that crazy baby, go look downstairs." Turning around, I ran down the stairs and followed the sounds of singing coming from the living room. Stepping in the room, I stood there and watched my mom comb Sunny's hair while singing to her.

It was weird as hell because it was just yesterday, she was trying to snatch her ass and today she's acting like shit never happened. I cleared my throat to make them aware of my presence. "Hey mommy, Grandma wanted to comb my hair today. Is that ok?"

"Yes baby, that's fine." Sitting on the couch, I watched as she talked and laughed with my daughter. Something that she had never done with her own child. When she finished, I sent Sunny upstairs to her room. As soon as I saw she was out of the room and couldn't hear me, I spoke up.

"What the fuck are you doing?" I spat with my voice laced with hate.

"I'm just trying to do what's right. The Lord dealt with me all last night and I couldn't wake up this morning still being on the same shit as yesterday. I want to tell you that I am sorry, and I was wrong for what I tried to do. You don't have to forgive me but just know, I'm going to try to be a better person and to be around more for you and my grand baby." Not knowing how to receive that shit, so I frowned up at her.

"Don't be with no shit mama, for real. It's cool to play with me cause I've learned to deal with the lies and you turning your back on me. Sunny isn't used to that and I don't want you to do all of this just to go back home and not even see the girl again."

"Just let me show you." She assured me that she was going to try to do better. I wasn't about to let my guard down completely, but just enough for her to show me if her true colors are trying to show through this façade.

"See, I told you she wasn't crazy enough to try that shit again." Bell announced as he walked into the room.

"Oh, I'm fasho crazy, I just wouldn't do anything like that again. I repented and I rebuke all of that foolishness, in the name of Jesus. Listen, when the good Lord came to me in my sleep last night, he wouldn't even let me in the gates of Heaven. I saw Snow standing on the other side of the gate with a sign that read, *How you gone hate from outside the gates, when you can't even get in?*

The next thing I know, the clouds open under my feet and I was falling to hell. That shit was hotter than that thang and I was not trying to take my ass down there for real. So, I'm here! I'm trying, and I'm sorry." She let out in a slow voice as if she was getting chocked up.

Looking over at Bell, he threw his arms up as if he were staying out of it. Turning back around, I looked at her to see if I could tell if she was actually being honest.

"Let me prove it to you. Y'all go out and do whatever you have to do, and I'll keep Sunny. Just leave us some money and the keys to one of those nice ass whips outside," she grinned with her hand out.

"With your face all beat up like that, you may want to stay inside" I advised.

"Girl please, I'm about to go to the dollar store and get me some good make up and cover all this shit up. It's cold as hell out but we still about to get out in these streets. With the help of my new son in law and his fat pockets. Judging by how big this house is, I know he got some deep pockets too."

"Ma!" I blurted out because I couldn't believe she said that.

"It's cool baby." Bell told me before going into his pocket. "Here is some money and here are all of the numbers to call Lyft, Uber and a Taxi service. You will not drive none of my cars or trucks."

"It's cool son in law. You gotta warm up to me so I ain't even mad about you being stingy right now."

"That's not being stingy." I told her. She was really tripping like someone was really about to hand her over some keys to something she couldn't afford to fix if she fucked it up.

"How about I get my brother to put some gas in your car and bring it over here to you?" Bell suggested.

"I guess that could work." She didn't seem excited about having to drive something that's hers. "Oh, and it's plenty food, water and backyard for y'all to play in and bond." Agreeing with him, I waved bye and told them to call me if they needed me. At first, I wasn't fucking with her, but I was willing to try as long as she was showing me that she was trying to change.

"Let's go so my brother can stop calling me. He say Sasha is not answering the room phone or the cell phone I gave her."

"She must have really put it on his ass to make him act like this already?" I asked as he helped me get in the truck.

"I guess so. The last I heard, she found out that he was my brother and accused him of killing her mom. Then a little while later, I received a text saying he was headed home, and he got the draws."

"I still don't want to believe that because Sasha is so sweet, and she just doesn't seem like that type of woman who would-"

"Give it up that easily?" He finished.

"Exactly. So, Tim needs him to stop capping on his dick."

"You've only known shorty for a few weeks now. You can't say what someone will or won't do if the opportunity presents itself. How about whatever they did, we just stay out of their business. We need to worry about us and making sure our shit is on point." Huffing loudly, I agreed to not say shit and just wait until she said something to me.

We pulled out of the garage and headed towards the express way. Today, Bell told Sasha that we would let her pick out the house she and the girls wanted to stay in. I could only imagine how hard it was for her to accept anything from him because of the feelings she had towards him. From what they've both told me, it seemed like an accident and really shouldn't be put all on them. Bell could have easily said that too, but I do commend him for still trying to make things right with her.

Looking down on my lap, I ran my hand across the new Chanel bag that Bell bought me last week and smiled. If you would have told me weeks ago that my daughter and I would be living in this big ass house, riding in these nice ass cars, I would have told you to bet money on it because I knew you were going to lose.

I had no idea that things would get turned around for me so quickly. Bell made me trust him and actually believe that he was going to do right by us. Dates became a routine for us and he made sure we went on one every other day.

Once we moved in with him, Sunny and I were pampered from head to toe. He also made sure we got a complete checkup. I didn't even get offended by that part because we were literally on the streets at one point and we could have come in contact with anything.

We got showered with gifts daily and at night, he would give me the gift of dick until the sun started shining through the windows. Bell didn't just talk about being a great man for us, he actually did it. "You gone rub the leather off that bag if you keep on rubbing it like that," Bell announced, gaining my attention.

"Sorry, I was in a daze."

"What's on your mind?" He quizzed

"Life." I let out with a sigh.

"What's wrong with your life? You are finally back to where you used to be, if not in a better position than you used to be in. If it's something wrong, what can I do to help make it better?" My phone started going off before I had a chance to tell him that nothing was wrong with me.

"Hello," I answered.

"Um yes, is this Snow Daye?" an older gentleman asked.

"Yes, may I ask who am I speaking with?"

"Yes, this is attorney Alan Tucker. I'm calling on behalf of the Cook County Hospital for the patient of Devin McAuthor. I'm sure you are aware of his passing due to hospital negligence."

"Oh my, no I didn't hear that. You said he passed away because of something the hospital did?" I was lying my ass off. I knew his ass was dead and that's exactly where he needed to be too.

"Yes ma'am. One of the nurses administered too much medicine and it stopped his heart. His body started to decompose rapidly so they had to go ahead and cremate him. I know this may be a bad time to talk about this but Ms. Daye, the hospital does know they made a big mistake. They are prepared to offer you a large settlement to avoid a lawsuit and more negative publicity. Since you are the only kin Devin has close to him, this offer is for you to either agree or disagree to."

"Yea, what's that amount?" While I waited to see what he was about to say, I put him on mute to let Bell know who was on the phone.

"Hurry up and get back on before that nigga hang up." He spat, making me laugh.

"Ms. Daye," Mr. Tucker called out to me.

"Yes, I'm here," I answered anxiously.

"The first amount they offered is 1.4 million dollars."

"1.4 mill-"

"However, we are willing to offer a final settlement of 4.5 million dollars. This offer is available provided you agree to an indemnity agreement that you will not file suit or take other legal actions against the against the hospital or the employee."

"Ok, I understand. Just tell me where and when I need to meet you so I can sign the paperwork. I won't sue and they can do whatever they want with his remains because I really have no use for them." I didn't want that shit laying around my house collecting dust.

"Tomorrow morning at 9 a.m. That will give me enough time to get the paperwork in order for you." I wrote down his address quickly and ended the call.

"What he say?"

"Daaang nosy!" I joked.

"Oh really? Niggas get a little bit of money and want to start acting funny."

"Whatever nigga! First off, it's a lotta bit of money and I was just joking with you. I have to be at his office in the morning and the hospital is giving me a check in the amount of 4.5 million fucking dollaaaars!!" I started dancing in my seat as I screamed out loudly.

"Cool, that should have you and shorty straight for a little minute. I guess you don't need me no more huh?" My eyebrows snapped together fast when he let that shit roll off his tongue.

"Why would you say something like that? I'm not with you for your money. What you give me, is just what you give me. Don't try to make it seem like I only used you, cause that was not the case at all. It's fucked up for you to even say something like that." When we first met, I didn't even want to accept a hotel room from his ass, and I was living in a shelter. How dare he even insinuate something so fucking wrong.

"You're right, I'm sorry about that. It was wrong of me and I apologize. Do you forgive a nigga or what Snow?"

"I guess, just don't let that shit happen again. Got it?" Gripping his chin, I pulled his face close to mine and bit his bottom lip.

"Ouch, shit! Calm yo lil ass down." When we pulled up to the hotel, Bell came around and opened the door for me to get out.

"What the hell?" I blurted out as a car came speeding up on us fast followed by the loud screeching sound of their tires trying to stop immediately.

"I thought I was late. I'm glad I made it here on time." Tim jumped out the car, with a bouquet of roses and two bears in his hand.

"Dang, her pussy must've been good as fuck. Got cho ass acting like a hype." Bell taunted him as they dapped each other up. I walked ahead to let them talk and also so I could talk to Sasha before Tim came into the room. I needed to know if that shit was true or not. She could have at least made his ass wait like I did. Although, my day dream felt good as hell, we still didn't touch each other for two weeks. I needed that shit too, it was just too much of him walking around being untouched. When he did give me some, he really gave me that shit. I'm talking bout, toes popping, heart beating rapidly, sweat dropping, ass cheeks bouncing, and all. It was everything I imagined it to be.

"Who is it?" Sasha called out as I knocked on the room door.

"It's me, Snow." She opened the door with a big ass smile on her face.

"Hey boo! Come inside. Excuse the mess, the doorman bought the girls some slime to make and we have stuff everywhere."

"It's ok, you guys won't be here much longer anyway," I advised.

"Where's Bell?"

"Outside talking to Tim." Just the mention of his name made her eye lashes flutter. "What was that all about?"

"Huh? What?"

"That expression you gave when I mentioned him. Did something happen between you two?" I was going to play dumb until her ass told me the truth.

"Yea, I found out that his ass was Bell's brother so of course, I got pissed off about my mom all over again."

"Sasha, listen to me when I tell you this and no way am I taking up for them and disregarding how you feel at all. But, have you actually sat back and thought about that day? Like what happened, how it happened, and if everything truly does fall on them?"

"YES! Why else would I have so much hate towards them if I didn't have a reason."

"Wow!" I expressed because that really threw me for a loop.

"So let me get this straight. You actually hate Bell and Tim for what happened to your mom?"

"Correct!"

"Then why are you up in his shit then? If I hated a person, I wouldn't want shit from them. The way you said it, it's not the type of hate you have when you dislike the taste of grape pop. No, that was the sound of someone who wants revenge."

"Correct again. Why wouldn't I get all that I could get out of them? Bell is ready and willing to drop off as much cash as I need to make our lives better. Tim is willing to pay for all of the therapy I need and, he's dropping off dick too." I couldn't believe what she was saying.

"That's some low-down shit, Sasha. Plus, I went and read the story of what happened, and the bus driver was charged with your moms' death. They gave you a settlement and you were awarded a nice amount of money. You never told me that part. What did you do with the money?"

"I didn't have to tell you shit, Snow. Yes, they charged him because he was driving under the influence but that doesn't justify the reason why she was running in the first place. She would have never gotten hit, if they wouldn't have taken the money that she had in her hand. She would have never gotten hit if-"

"She would have looked both ways, or if the driver wasn't under the influence. Honestly, this isn't their fault, it's the drivers. You still never said what happened to the money that they awarded you for her death."

"What fucking money are you talking about Snow? I was young as hell when it happened, they weren't given me any money, so I don't know what happened to it. If I had it, I wouldn't have struggled so fucking hard with my auntie and uncle. If I had it, I wouldn't have been on the streets either."

"So, you never went and got the money when you turned 18?"

"Can you hear? I just said I never got any money nor did my auntie tell me about any money." My eyes bucked out and I looked around the room for her things.

"Bitch get up, you got an I.D right?"

"Yea, Snow what are you doing?" Tossing her coat to her, I ran in the other room and helped the girls put on theirs.

"Listen, if you never picked the money up, that means it's still money to be picked up. Let's go get that shit. It shouldn't be hard for them to look up the case and see that you were awarded money that you never received."

"Shit girl, fuck them kids; let's go." Laughing, I grabbed the girls and rushed out the door. The elevator seemed like it was taking forever to open up, once it finally did Bell and Tim tried to step out. Pushing them back inside, I explained on the way back down what Sasha needed to do. For some reason, they both looked pissed after I told them about the drunk driver.

Bell said back then, he didn't try to read a damn newspaper to find out everything. He just asked his mom to find out when the lady that got hit by the bus funeral was and she did. Even as an adult, he never tried to go back and read cause in his mind, nothing was different from what he knew. I think he was pissed at the fact that he beat himself up for something that wasn't really his fault. I have no idea what Tim was over there with the stale face for.

"Hey Mr. Tim." Angel spoke shyly.

"Hey girls," he waved back, "ay, Nevaeh, ask yo mama why she ignored my calls this morning?"

Doing as she were told, she asked, "Hey ma, Mr. Tim said, why were you ignoring him this morning.".

"Tell Mr. Tim because I was pissed the fuck off and didn't want to be bothered."

"Mr. Tim, my mama said mind yo daaaamn business bitch. She ain't wanna answer the phone for you because you don't know 2+2, dumb ass bitch." I think we were all so shocked at her talking like that, that we were quiet as hell.

"Oh, now you know I'm about to beat cho ass right? You know damn well I do not talk like." Reaching for Nevaeh's arm, she pulled her close to her and attempted to spank her. That attempt failed because Tim stopped her.

"Don't whoop her for that, it's my fault. When we were in the truck heading here last night, I didn't have any kid movies, so I just turned Kevin Hart on and gave them headphones," he admitted.

"Nigga, are you crazy?" Sasha blurted out.

"Ok, that's enough. I don't know what you two need to hash out, but y'all need to do it fast because I'm tired of it. You guys are acting like some kids with this back and forth stuff. Sasha, like I told you in the room, this shit is not their fault and you know it.

I don't know what Tim is trying to do but shit you already gave up the goodies so what's the point of acting funny with him now? Leave all of this mess alone and work on getting your life back on the right track. It's sad what happened to your mom but let's not make this the reason why you continue to miss out on great things." I was tired of the shit with them and I had only around them for a few minutes.

It's like Sasha was looking for someone to blame for the shit that she went through in life. Honestly, they aren't the reason her aunt and uncle did her wrong. They aren't the reason, she ended up back in a shelter with her girls. Sometimes you have to know when to let go of the past. Especially, when it's only fucking your life up more by holding on to shit that happened a century plus more ago.

"I don't mean any harm Snow, but you don't get to tell me how or when to let something go," Sasha snapped back.

"You're right, but what have holding on to it gotten you?" When I asked that, she paused for a long time. "We are standing out here in the cold wasting time, just going back and forth. As your friend, I'm just trying to help you get things back together. Someone was able to help me, so why wouldn't I want to do the same for you?"

"You're right, and I'm sorry. I just-"

"Don't even worry about explaining it. You had your reasons and we are just going to move on at this point, ok?" I questioned.

"Ok. Thank you." Nudging her arm, she smiled before giving me a hug. "Tim, do you mind if the girls and I ride with you to the courthouse?"

"Nah, I just need to swing by Walmart to find them some more suitable movies to watch back there. I can't have them turning to little bad ass sour patch kids on my watch." Laughing, she helped the girls in the truck as I turned to get back inside the truck with Bell.

"Call and check on your mom and Sunshine. Make sure her ass ain't got her out in this damn cold." Bell told me right as I got inside of the truck. Grabbing my phone out of my purse, I called my mom's phone to check on my baby.

"Yea!" she answered with a lot of noise in the background.

"What's going on? What's all of that noise?"

"Baby girl wanted to have a party for all of the birthday's I missed. I was being nosey and found a stack of money Bell left out for me."

"Ma, Bell didn't leave any money out for you."

"It was in his closet, on the left hand side, wrapped in two blankets and stuffed in a book bag. That was definitely out there for me. I ordered her all types of clowns and inflatables. It's just us but the DJ is bumping hard."

"Ma! What the hell is wrong with you? For one, that wasn't your money, and for two, it's too damn cold to be outside in some damn inflatables. What dummy even came over to do that shit for you?" I asked.

"Your brother! He got his own company and once I told him how much I would pay, he blew that shit up with his mouth." I ran my hand down my face, while shaking my head.

Letting out a deep sigh, I told her, "Don't touch shit else and get all of those clowns and your son out of the house. We didn't want your ass there so what made you think we wanted anyone else there?"

"You've always been a stick in the mud. I thought you might have changed since you were with the rich nigga and all. Anyway, I gotta go rambling again. I could really make a come up and buy my own house right next door. I just needed to search a little harder for the rest of the money he left out for me."

"MA!" I called out before the call ended.

Looking over at Bell, I was too ashamed to even say

what she had done.

"She got two more days!" Was all he said before

I even told him anything. Dropping the phone back in

my purse, I glanced out of the window right as we were

going pass the shelter. Shit had been so crazy since

Christmas that I hadn't even made time to go by there

yet. I had so many plans for that place and I couldn't

wait to get them rolling by the New Year.

Fifteen minutes later, we were arriving at the

courthouse. Sasha and I got out of the trucks while they

all stayed inside. As we walked in, we found the first

available person then walked to her window. Sasha

explained here situation and kept putting emphases on

the part about it was a check here for her. The lady told us to hold on while she stepped away for a second.

"I really hope they still have it here and they didn't void it after all of these years."

"I'm sure they can reprint another one," I told her.

"Now that you've helped me see the truth, I don't even feel right taking money from Bell anymore. Even though he really wants to help, I just can't do it," Sasha stated.

The lady came back with some papers in her hand then gave them to Sasha. Judging by the look that was on her face, I knew something was all fucked up. "I'm sorry Ms. Barrett, but we sent out a letter to the address on that paper. We informed your guardian that you had a check that was giving to you for the death of your mom. A lady by the name of Daisy Smith, came up here and signed for it.

I remember her because she opened the envelope right here and started turning flips in the lobby. This had to be about seven years ago. At the time, she was still your guardian and there wasn't much we could do once she showed the proof. I'm sorry. I wish there were more that I could do." I stared at Sasha as tears began filling up in her eyes. She thanked the lady for her help and started walking out the door. Running to catch up with her, I stopped her from walking and pulled her into a hug.

"I'm sorry Sasha. I was really hoping it would still be here for you."

"It's ok. This is just the life that I'm supposed to live, that's all. I'll figure all of this out on my own."

"No, you won't. You have all of us and you have those girls that you have to keep pushing for." I was trying to give her something positive but honestly, I would have been fucked up behind this too. "What do you want to do now?"

"Go see my aunt," she told me firmly. "Seven years ago, is when I had Angel. Her stupid ass already had that fucking check when she kicked us out of the house. That's what really made all of this so fucked up." Storming off, she jumped back in the truck with Tim. Within minutes, he was pulling off full speed. I'm guessing she made him aware of what happened.

"What they doing?" Bell asked me.

"Just follow them, your brother may need you to get him out of jail if they get over there and her auntie still at this house. That heffa had the nerve to come get that girl check then kick her out the house. That was some low down dirty shit. At this point, I'm willing to let you pay to get my hair done again, if I mess it up while beating her auntie ass with her."

"The fuck! Yo ass is getting out of hand. You better shoot her and wear that hair style another month. I just paid $450 for bundles, I had to pay to get that shit put in and now you want to go fuck it up. Matter fact, you have hair. Why do you keep putting that shit in your head anyway?"

"Now you are asking too many questions. Just keep up with them before you lose 'em and Sasha ends up getting all of the good licks in." Shaking his head, he sped up to catch up with them. I know this was the wrong prayer to say but I really prayed that her auntie was still here so she could tear into her ass.

CHAPTER 6 SASHA

I sat quietly as Tim followed the directions that I put into the GPS to get us to my aunt's house. My mind was running fast as hell with so many thoughts of what I wanted to do to her. When I saw the amount of money she picked up, my heart shattered. My daughters and I could have had a good fucking life.

I know she was only being spiteful because her husband was fucking me but shit, what was I supposed to do? As a kid, this nigga made it seem like the shit was my form of repayment since he allowed my auntie to take me in. I wasn't trying to go back on the streets, so I shut my mouth and did as he told me. Do I regret not saying thing to her sooner? Most definitely, and it's not because the hoe took all of my money, but because maybe that would have prevented me having another kid by his nasty ass. Not that I regret my girls, but it was hard living with the fact that I was raising daughters that were conceived by my uncle.

"You straight?" Tim reached his hand over and placed it on top of mine.

"I will be. I'm only going over here just to let her know that I know what she did. I'm sure that money is long gone by now. She probably smoked that shit up or decked her house out in some old ass furniture with white fur throws on couches and shit."

"Just know, regardless of the outcome, I still want us to be good. I know I pushed up on you quick as hell and hardly knew you," he stated with embarrassment coiled around him.

"Right, you did." I interrupted.

"So, let me take the time to get to know you then. I'm really a good dude, Sasha. My last relationship was like three years ago. Not because I couldn't find anyone, but I wanted to focus on me and get myself to the point where I had more to offer to my woman besides good d-i-c-k," he spelled it out then looked in the mirror to make sure the girls did hear him. They had headphones on anyway so they wouldn't have heard him.

"For me, it was just really weird that you even looked at me twice."

"Why though? You didn't look homeless so the only thing I saw was a beautiful woman that I wanted to get to know. That's usually how things start out, right? You see a woman that catches your eye, and you do everything to make her see you and want to give you a chance.

I just don't want this situation to make you push away from us because my brother and I will still do all that we can to make sure you and those girls are good. Can we make a promise that you won't pull away?" Holding his pinky finger out, he put it close to mine. "Promise me." I hesitated a little bit because I didn't really know what would happen after this. I wasn't trying to seem like a charity case so hell yea, I may run away from if shit goes bad here. "Sasha!" he called out, pulling me out of my thoughts.

"Yes! Yea! I promise." Locking my pinky into his, I took a deep breath then exhaled. Giving him a half smile, before turning my head to look out the window.

"Mommy, what does condemn mean?" Nevaeh asked as she looked out the window and read what was posted all over the house. Getting out the truck, my heart sunk into my stomach as I looked at this abandon house. She must have been gone for years, because this place was a mess.

"I'll check the mailbox to see if anything still comes here." Snow told me as she walked up.

"Hey! Are you the new tenants? I can't believe she's trying to rebuild and rent out that mess." Hearing an old lady's voice, we all turned around and saw a lady hanging out the window next door.

"No, my auntie Daisy used to live here. Do you know where she is now?" I asked her.

"Yep, she moved on up to the upper east side. She told me that her big sister left her some insurance money and she could finally move out of the ghetto. I was a little offended cause my house is not in the ghetto. In fact, it's the best-looking house on the block."

Her house looked like it should have caution tape all around it. I don't know if she was a hoarder or what but she had six toilets lined up on the side of her house. Containers of newspapers on her porch, and bags of garage just there taking up space. Something smelled like shit, the closer we walked to her house. "Give me a minute to get out there." Leaving from the window, we heard a lot of noise and things being thrown before she appeared at the front door.

"I don't mind taking you guys to her new house. Just let me put some clothes on first." She stepped outside and started moving the bags that were on the porch. The same bags that I assumed were bags of garbage.

"Damn!" Tim blurted out while we covered their nose and mouths. She tore opened one of the bags and the smell of horse shit came flying out. After she fiddled through the clothes, she finally found what she was looking for. "I hope she don't think her nasty ass getting in my truck. I would never be able to get that smell out my seats." Tim told us after she went back inside of the house.

"She gone have to get her ass on the hood or something cause she ain't getting in my shit either. Matter fact, let me call her ass an Uber now and we can just follow them," Bell suggested before pulling his phone out.

"I'm ready." She stepped out with her wig twisted and her clothes on, inside out. "I'll need one of you handsome men to run me by the bank."

"I got you a car on the way right now. We didn't expect anyone to ride with us so both of our trucks are full." Bell told her.

"We got room next to us-" Angel announced before Nevaeh covered her mouth up quickly.

"Mind yo daaamn business bitch," she whispered to her and I had to make a mental note to talk to her about that shit. Even though, we all wanted to say the same thing; her little butt should not be talking like that.

"Oh, ok. Well I'm Ms. Shelton." She reached her hand out to us and we all just gave her ass the head nod. Moments later, the Uber driver was pulling up and we could tell by the expression on his face once she got inside that he was pissed off. We all got inside of the trucks and followed them to Daisy's house.

It took us about 30 minutes to pull up to where she lived out in County Club Hills. I was impressed and pissed the fuck off at the same damn time at how nice her house looked. Getting out, I walked up to the door and started knocking hard as hell. Every time I knocked; Tim would kick the door.

"This nigga about to go to jail," Bell said.

"Who the fuck is knocking at my door like this?" The door flew open and aunt Daisy stepped out in this white silk gown with a white silk robe covering her up. "Bitch, how did you find me?" She asked before looking around and noticing Ms. Shelton on the other side of the screen door. "Oh, no! You are not bringing that smell in my damn house. Stay yo ass over there." She told her as she took a long pull on her Newport.

"Where in the fuck is my money?" I blurted out, getting right to the point.

"Where the fuck is my money from taking care of you and my great niece slash step kids? What did I look like rewarding the bitch who was fucking my husband? After all that I was doing for you, you let my husband knock you up; twice!" My heart started beating fast as hell and a wave of emotions took over me.

"Bitch your husband was raping me. Don't try to act like I was just out here fucking him. I was fifteen years old, fifteen! You were supposed to protect me but yet you were never home. You mistreated me and his ass made it seem like he was the one doing everything for me. He made me pay him back in pussy and that's something you should have taken up with him. He knew he was wrong but yet, you are still married to him."

"Says who? I let his ass go just like I let yo ass go. Now what do you want? I have shit to do," she paused then looked over at Ms. Shelton, "and you smell like shit. You really need to burn down that damn house of yours."

"Oh, I smell like shit, well watch this." Before we could react, Ms. Shelton was pushing past aunt Daisy and rushing into her house. We stood at the door and watched as she rolled and sat down on all of her white furniture. Daisy ran behind her with air freshener, spraying down everything she touched.

"Not my bed!" Daisy yelled out. I took this time to rambling through her purse that was on the table by the door. Finding a check book, I flipped through it and saw the balance that was left as of yesterday. 100,000 wasn't shit compared to what she had previously but I was about to take all of this shit out. I told Tim to go get

her from upstairs and put her in the truck. We were

taking this bitch right to the bank to withdraw all of this

money.

I thought about writing a check to myself and

cashing it, but that evil bitch, would have stopped the

check. Hearing fumbling coming from the stairs, Ms.

Shelton came tumbling down with a hand full of sheets

as she ran out of the door. To be an old lady, she was

getting around fast as hell. Tim and Daisy came down

next and I knew it had to be a reason she wasn't fighting

against him. I didn't find out what it was until they

walked out the front door. He had a gun pressed into her

back, forcing her to keep walking.

"I'll take the girls back home with me to play

with Sunshine. You can just come over once you get

everything together and we can just go from there."

Snow went to the truck and got the girls out before Daisy and Tim made to the backseat. They pulled off and I slid in the back with Daisy while keeping the gun trained on her. I didn't know how to really use I.T but I knew pulling the trigger would kill her ass and that's all I needed to know.

"Oh, you think you a boss chick now? I wonder how much you had to sleep with this young man for to make him want to do all of this for you. My ex-husband said you had some power between your legs which is why he couldn't let you go." The more she spoke the more furious I had gotten. I knew I couldn't hit her ass in the mouth because they would think something if she walked into the bank beat up.

I'm gone let her ass make it until I get the rest of

my money, then I'll beat the hoe ass. Pulling up to the

bank, I got out with her and told her to withdraw

everything out the bank or I was going to have Tim kill

her. He really wasn't, but she didn't know that shit.

Doing as she were told, she withdrew the money and told

them it was to pay off the rest of her house. I didn't give

a damn what she told them; I just wanted my coins.

Well, what was left of it.

We got back in the truck and drove off. "I hope

you feel really good about yourself now, stealing from

your own auntie."

"I feel just about as good as you did when you

stole from your own niece; now get out." Pushing the

back door open, I kicked her out of the truck while it was

moving and prayed someone ran her ass over.

"Damn! Why you ain't tell me to pull over?"

"Now what fun would that have been?" I replied to Tim as I sat back and counted my money with a smile on my face.

CHAPTER 7 TIM

"What now?" I probed while she flipped through the money for the tenth time.

"What now? I try to get a little bit of what I lost back. I mean, I promised my girls that once I got some money, I was going to buy us a mansion. I've always wanted an all-white Range Rover. We need knew clothes, shoes, furniture for our mansion, and I haven't had my hair done in forever, so I'm definitely getting me some good ass weave."

"Whoa! I think you counted that money too many times. That's only 100 racks in your hand Sasha. You ain't getting half of that stuff with only 100 racks; especially not a mansion. A truck is doable, but I don't think you need to spend that much right now. Not until you get on your feet and have steady income coming in. You have to be smart.

If Bell offered you a place to live, then take it. That's one thing knocked off your list that you don't have to take out of your money. Get the clothes and shoes y'all need but just don't go out and do nothing crazy and end up back in the situation you were in before." I was trying to help her out but the way she was smelling that money; I knew my words were going in one ear and out the other.

"You sound like a hater on the front line. Why would I not go out and splurge a little bit? I've been dusty for years now and it's time that I upgrade myself just a little bit." I dropped the subject and focused back on the road. She was about to do some dumb shit and at this point, she wouldn't be able to blame no one but herself. "I promise not to go crazy as long as you promise to not hurt me if I allow you to get to know me better. As you can see, my taste in men has not been the best by far. I'm not trying to rush anything though so let's grow as friends and whatever happened from there just happen. Deal?"

"I'm cool with that. Just know that your past circumstances don't define who you are today. The past is just that, and we're trying to get you to something better than you had before. Don't think I was trying to control you when I was telling you to think smart, I was just looking out for you. The last thing you want to do, is end up back where you started." She agreed with me and also promising that she'll do right, and not start living hood rich. I hoped like hell that shit was true but only time will tell.

Pulling up to the house, we picked up the girls and headed back out. Since all of that shit happened today, they put off finding a place to stay until later but for now, she will just stay at the hotel. Once we got the girls, she wanted to go to the mall and buy them some new clothes. I was cool with that because I ain't have shit to do anyway.

I gotta meet my brother Prince but whatever he wanted to talk about could wait till later. Parking, we got out and headed inside the mall. The first stop was The Children's Place, and she damn near bought two of everything in the store. The girls were having the time of their lives trying on their clones and shoes.

"Mr. Tim, how do I look?" Angel asked as she came out of the dressing room in this pink top, black leggings and a black and pink tutu.

"Like a damn snitch," Nevaeh blurted out as she came out the dressing room in the exact same thing.

"Vaeh, you better watch your mouth and I'm serious. I don't know what has gotten into you but I'm not having it. Cut it out now!" Sasha scolded making Neveah drop her head as if she were sad. "I don't know what happened to my sweet little girls." Sasha stated to me while looking through another rake of clothes.

"They are still there. It could be worse though so be happy that you can still correct it now and it's nothing serious. Well, nothing too serious anyway." Nodding her head, she turned away from me so she could take the girls more clothes. While I waited, I looked through the clothes so I wouldn't look like a weirdo just standing by the kids dressing room.

"Tim? Is that you?" Turning around, my eyes locked with this chick name Natalie. In high school, I had the biggest crush on her but she was two grades above me and she wasn't checking for me. I used to see her in gym all the time but she always ignored my ass. She was so beautiful to me and not much has changed about her since back then. Her light pale complexion covered in freckles still looked smooth. She always wore her hair in a short style back then so to see it long and bone straight was different.

My eyes roamed her body several times before I even acknowledged her. Here I was stuck in a daze like I was that sixteen-year-old kid again.

"I'm sorry, I must have the wrong person," she announced before she turned away from me.

"Natalie, my bad I just got caught up, it's been a while. How have you been?"

"I've been good. I didn't know if that was you or not 'cause it's been so long since I've seen you. You look really good. What are you doing now?"

"Nothing much, I own a couple business. Just trying to do anything to stay out of trouble." She smiled and gave me a little laugh before tossing her hair over her shoulder.

"You were never the type to get in trouble, so I don't know what you're talking about."

"How would you know? You barely looked at me."

"Just because I never said anything to you, doesn't mean I didn't know who you were. How do you think I know your name and still remembered your face?"

"Probably because I still look good as fuck; just like I did back then. Even if you didn't know my name, you still would remember the fine ass young nigga from 5th period gym class." She let out a cute ass laugh as I stood there stuck staring her again.

"So conceited, just like your brothers. Anyway, it was nice catching up with you, I have to find my son before he throws everything in my cart. Who are you here shopping for?"

"Oh, no one! I'm here alone." I replied quickly.

"Sooo you're just standing by the kids dressing room... just cause?"

"Well no, I'm here with someone but I was just giving them a ride." That came out bad as hell but as usual, I always fumbled over what to say when it came to Natalie.

"I didn't know Uber drivers followed people inside the store too."

"Oh, you got jokes. I make too much money to be an Uber driver. I was just bringing a friend here to get somethings." I looked her up and down again before going into my pocket to pull out my card. "We should catch up later."

"That would be nice." Her pale cheeks, turned a blushing shade of red as she smiled at me. "I should be going now. I know my son is somewhere tearing this place apart." Taking the card from my hand, she smiled then walked back to the other side of the store. I looked around just in time to see Sasha walking out of the door. Confused, I rushed out behind her to catch up. I was so caught up in my conversation with Natalie that I didn't even see them walk past me.

"Ay, Sasha!" I called out to her but she kept walking off and pulling the girls with her. "Sasha!" I called again, stopping her in her tracks.

"What?" she asked with an attitude.

"What's wrong? Why you just walk out like that?"

"You were in there alone, right? So why does it matter why I left you? Go back and talk to your little friend, we'll find a ride back to the hotel," she spat before turning back around and heading for the door. I felt bad as hell for saying that shit now. Running my hand down my face, I followed her out the door. "I told you I was good!" she shouted.

"And I just want to make sure of that. I'll leave once I see whose picking you guys up. Or, you can just ride with me and I'll take y'all back to the hotel."

"Nah, we're good! Our ride will be here shortly. We won't need a ride from you anymore either. I'm going to go online and buy me a car from the vending machine thing and you won't have to worry about us anymore." Laughing, I reached for her bags and she pulled them back.

"Come one Sasha, quit tripping. Let me take you back to the hotel." I damn near begged.

"Nah, the uber driver is coming and he's going to take us to Carvana to get us a car. I'm not about to be around anyone who's ashamed to be around me."

"I'll take you to a real car lot if it's that serious, you don't have to go to a place like that. Who the fuck buys a car out of a vending machine anyway?" I asked her.

"A bitch with no credit and a purse full of money. B3 gone bring down a nice ass Mercedes Truck with low miles on it." Realizing she was serious, I stopped trying to fight against her and just waited on the driver to pull up. Once he did, I went and got into my truck and headed to my brother's crib. I would reach back out to her soon but as of now, I'll give her some space.

Picking my phone up, I sent Prince a text letting him know that I was on my way over. He told me he had some heavy shit to talk about and needed some advice. I wasn't the type of muthafucka who was good at giving advice about certain things. He knows that though and for him to still ask me, let's me know it must be some serious ass shit.

Getting out the truck, I hustled up the steps and let myself in. The sound of ass clapping and moaning came from the kitchen, so I took my ass right that way to see what bitch he had up in here today.

"Wow!" I dragged, "Now y'all know this some fucked up ass shit and I don't want no parts of it. Just know when he finds out, he gone kill both of y'all." Looking between both, I turned around and headed into the living room. About twenty minutes later, he walked her to the door. When he leaned in to give her a kiss, I knew this nigga had lost all of his mind. He was most definitely about to lose his life too. "You know you gone get cho ass beat, right?" I asked Prince, as he came into the living room.

"Bruh, that's where you come in at. How you let someone close to you know that you been smashing his girl?" The fact that he was dead ass serious was the part that fucked me up the most.

"Nah, I ain't got shit to do with shit. I don't even know why you called me over here knowing she would be here. They say you're supposed to pick your battles but your simple ass went right out there and deliberately picked a battle that you know you won't be able to fight. That shit foul, P." Getting up from the couch, I grabbed my keys off the table then headed out the door. I didn't even give him a chance to justify this shit cause the ass whooping he gone get, is one he deserves.

Just as fast as I pulled up to his crib, I pulled off even faster. I ain't want no parts in that bullshit. I hit a few blocks trying to think of shit to get into, but my mind kept wondering off to Sasha. I wasn't trying to have shorty mad at me over that shit that happened at the mall, but I wasn't gone press her. As bad as I wanted to pull up on her, I took my ass to the crib instead. Seems like staying out of shit was the best place for me right now.

Hitting the remote to let my garage up, I pulled in and got out. Soon as I stepped into the house, my line started buzzing.

"Yea!" I answered

"Can I come over?" She didn't even have to say her name because I could recognize that voice from anywhere. It's only a voice that I fantasized about moaning my name for years now.

"Hell yea, shorty! I'll send you my address," I expressed quickly.

"Cool. See you soon."

"Aight, don't wear no panties either," I blurted out as she was ending the call. Tossing the phone to the side, I went to my room and jumped in the shower. We not gone fuck, but I needed these balls to be clean just in case she wanted to sniff, suck and slob on my dick.

CHAPTER 8 BELL

Since we put off Sasha finding a place to say, I decided to take Snow out instead. It's rare that we have time to ourselves but since her mom was here, I may as well take advantage. I took her to one of her favorite restaurants and let her run up a tab. We must have sat and talked for over an hour before heading home to relax. Today had been long and eventful. All I wanted to do was come home to my quiet house and lay up with my girl. That shit wasn't gone happen though because as soon as we pulled in the driveway, it was a fucking circus in my yard. She must've found every stack of money I had hidden, to pull this shit off right here.

"What the fuck!" Snow mumbled as she saw all of the bullshit that her mama had going on. The fact that it was cold as fuck outside made this shit even worse.

"Wait Snow!" I called out as she opened the door before I had a chance to put the truck in park.

"You have to go and you need to do it right now. If you got this much energy to do all of this snooping and throwing unnecessary ass parties then you got enough energy to take yo ass home. You have managed to pop up and turn my life back the fuck upside down. I can't and I won't let you do this shit to me again. So, you and your son can get all of this shit and leave. Now!" Snow was furious and I didn't blame her one bit. I would usually stop her from going off on her mom, but this time she needed to do it.

"But Snow, I was-"

"No buts, ma! I don't even want to hear the lies because that's all you have been doing since you got her," she huffed. "All of this shit," Snow spun around pointing at all of the inflatables in my yard, "is just your way of doing something to get under my skin even more. When I come back out here, all of this shit better be gone and you need to be gone with it." Storming off, she went inside of the house and left all of us standing here looking stupid.

I knew she wasn't mad at me about shit, but her whole vibe had a nigga shook. "Bell, can you talk to her for me please. I was just trying to make my grand baby happy. If I had known, she would get this upset I wouldn't have done it. Please, you have to believe me. I'm really trying to be better than I used to be," she pleaded.

"I'll talk to her, just get this stuff cleaned up so she will be less pissed when she come back out." Nodding her head, she walked off and started talking to her son. He looked at me but ain't say shit, just started taking everything down. I ain't like the vibe of his ass but since he was about to leave, I wasn't gone address that shit.

Turning around, I headed inside of the house to see what Snow was doing. When I walked inside of the room, she was laying across the bed crying.

"Be easy baby," I told her as I pulled her off the bed and into my arms, "Everything that she messed up could easily be replaced. Don't let that shit fuck up your happiness. On top of that, you're about to go to the lawyer tomorrow and pick up a fat ass check just for you and your daughter to have your way with." I cupped her chin up from my chest so she could look at me, "Just enjoy this moment you have with her because pretty soon it will all be over.

I don't need you to be stressed out about shit. You also have a business to start running so clear your mind so everything can fall into place for you."

"I'm trying but everything seems like it's just hitting me all at once. I guess once I go see the lawyer tomorrow and get things squared away there, we can go by the shelter."

"You got the address of where you have to go to meet him?" I asked her.

"Yea, it's in my purse in the living room. I supposed to be there by 9 a.m. I'll get up early and take care of that then come back here to get you or either you can just meet me at the shelter."

"Sounds like a plan. Now stop pouting and go down there and get y'all situation handled. I'm about to step out for a bit, then I'll be back a little later on." Kissing her on the forehead, she then slipped out of my arms and headed down the stairs. After grabbing my keys to leave again, I looked to make sure they weren't fighting before I pulled off.

I have no idea what her mom's intentions are, but I don't plan on her being around here much longer. I've been trying to do all I can to get Snow back on the right track and I really don't want any distractions. Her mom is only going to add more bullshit for her to worry about instead of having her focus on the shit that's important.

Some kind of way, I gotta get rid of her mom, and I gotta do that shit before the New Year. My plans need to flow as smoothly as possible that day and I don't need no fuck ups from her mom.

Hearing a horn blow behind me, snapped me out of my thoughts. The light had already turned green, so I pulled off. My sister Cashmere has been blowing me up all day, so I needed to swing by her crib to make sure she was good. Knowing Cash, she's into some shit cause that's the only time she blows me up.

Pulling up to her crib, all of the lights were off but her cars were in the driveway, so I parked and got out.

Using my key, I let myself in and walked to the little flicker of light that I saw in the kitchen. I had my gun out the entire time 'cause something just didn't seem right. Flipping the lights on, I looked at Cash sitting at the kitchen table then started laughing. She was sitting there dressed in all black, with her big ass pit bull, Midnight, by her side.

"What the fuck you doing sis?" Before speaking again, she spit what looked like sunflower seeds out her mouth before beginning.

"I sealed the deal for you, and made it a dead deal. Now you have to repay me for my time, and my energy. These are my numbers." Sliding me a piece of paper, I opened it then looked back at her to make sure she was dead ass serious.

"What you want me to do with this, Cash?"

"I got blood on my hands for you and your girl. Did you think that shit was priceless? Big brother or not, I need my coins and I need them now." Taking off my coat, I took a seat at the other end of the table where she was sitting. Midnight started growling at me, so I shot his ass in the head before looking back at my sister.

"What the fuck! Midnight, get up baby! Bell why would you do that?"

"Why would you ask me for a fucking million dollars because you killed a muthafucka that I didn't ask yo ass to kill? The fucking dog looked mangy anyway and he needed to be put to sleep. Now, did I ask you for some money for that? No! Me killing your dog was a choice that I made. You doing whatever you did to dude, was a fucking choice. I'm not about to pay you a million dollars for some shit I could have done myself. You took it upon yourself to do that shit," I barked.

"Aight, what about two racks then? I need to pay my car off and that's all I need. If you give me that, I won't even take you to Judge Mathis for killing my dog.

Cause that was most definitely some crackhead shit.

Especially since Midnight didn't even do shit to you."

"Why couldn't you just ask for some money, instead of doing this dumb shit? I've never had a problem with given you, Sparkle, Monte, Tim or Prince, a damn thing. Don't ever try to play me like that, Cash."

"Ok, you right. On top of that 2 grand, can you buy me a new pit too? You know that was my baby."

"Yea, just don't pull no shit like that again. I'll put a little something in your account tomorrow," I told her as I got up from the table and started putting my coat back on.

"Bell, since we got that lil money issue out the way, I just thought I should be the one to let you know that Prince is fucking Yolanda." Pausing, I shook my head and left out the door without saying a word.

That shit with Prince is no surprise to me because I've always saw the way they used to joke and shit with each other. The shit didn't faze me because I never saw her as more than what she was. She wasn't my wife, or nothing close to that shit. What they do is what they do. I moved on to bigger shit and don't even have time to address nothing that doesn't concern me anymore.

Sliding back in my truck, I pulled off and headed back to the crib. I prayed they had their shit handled by now because all I want to do was spend some time with my girl and worry about us. Everybody else problems are off limits to us now. Muthafuckas do what they gotta do for them, so I'll make sure I do what I have to do for us.

CHAPTER 9 SNOW

"Mommy, where's grandma? She was just downstairs and for a second, I thought she was you." Sunny asked as she crawled in the bed with me.

"Really? She said she had something to do then she would come back to say goodbye to us. I didn't get a chance to see her before she left out the house though. She just spoke through the intercom system." I pulled her closer to me and wrapped her in my arms. "You know granny will be going home soon, so she won't be around here much anymore. Hopefully once she gets back home, she will keep in touch with us. I know you enjoyed spending time with her."

"Yep it was fun." she replied with a big smile. "While you were sleeping, she was in your closet looking for clothes. When she came out the bathroom, I called out your name but noticed it was her when she turned around. She had on everything of yours. From your name necklace that Mr. Bell bought you, down to your shoes with the red bottoms."

"What the hell? Are you sure?" I asked as I crawled out of bed to look through my jewelry. Sure enough, my necklace was gone. Why in the hell would she want to wear a necklace with my name on it?

"Mommy, your phone is ringing." Walking back over to the bed, I took a seat and took my phone off the charger.

"Hello." I answered quickly once I saw it Mr. Tucker calling back.

"Good morning Ms. Daye. I know we have a meeting scheduled for 9 a.m, but I was calling you because I have a lady in my office now who is claiming to be you."

"Say what?" I quizzed.

"The lady is a lot older than Mr. Devin, so I figured it wasn't you. I'm sending you a picture of her right now."

"Ok, thank you." I started getting dressed, while I waited on the picture to come through. Hearing the ding, I pulled the phone back from my ear and got pissed off when I saw my mom sitting there looking like the broke down version of me. How did she even know about the meeting? "That's my mom. Don't give her shit or tell her that I am on my way there."

"Yes, ma'am. I'll keep her here for you." Ending the call, I finished getting myself and Sunny ready. I kept racking my brain to remember how in the hell did she know about any of this. I only told Bell in the car and once we got home, he mentioned it but... fuck! Her ass must have been listening to our conversation through the intercom. Grabbing my daughter's hand, and my keys, I headed out the door. I couldn't believe she would do something so low like this. Just when I thought we were making shit right after last night, she goes and pulls this bullshit.

Bell went to the diner so I sent him a text letting him know what happened so he could meet me over there. It was going to take the act of God to get me off her ass. Since God wasn't coming back anytime soon,

Bell was the only person who could stop me from killing her trifling ass.

It took us twenty minutes to get to his office and by the time I got there, I was even more livid when I saw she drove Bell's, Aston Martin. She had all types of fucking nerves for all of the stunts she's been pulling over the past few days. The shit she was doing made no sense at all.

"Come on, baby." Grabbing Sunny by the hand, we both barged inside of the office. All I could hear was her cackling loud as hell, so I followed her voice. "Ma!" I shouted, making her jump.

"Oh shit!" she froze quicker than Anna off Frozen when she heard me call her name. "He- hey daughter. My beautiful sunshine on a rainy day. The bloomiest sunflower in a meadow of dead roses." She was trying to say anything to keep me off her ass.

"Did you really think he was just going to hand money to you?" I questioned.

"Well, yea! I actually did. I mean, you really don't need it. Bell has a lot of money stashed around the house and I'm sure it's even more in a safe or a bank."

"That's his money though ma. What he got stashed away, has nothing to do with me," I told her.

"I knew I should have raised you right. Listen, if you giving up the ass, then he needs to be giving up the cash. Ain't no ifs, ands, or buts about it. If you don't have rights to the money that I found, then he shouldn't be get to enjoy the treat between your legs." I couldn't believe how serious she was right now.

Running my hand down my face, I looked at the lawyer and said, "I'm sorry, I'll get her out of here so we can talk. Ma, let's go!" Pulling her arm, we headed right outside and luckily Bell was pulling up. He could hold her ass out here and make sure she stayed put.

"Lock her ass in the trunk or something, I can't even deal with her right now. You see she even stole your car."

"Come on now, ma. You already blew money yesterday that wasn't yours. Fucking with my car, is the quickest way to get cho ass hurt. I've been really respectful because you are my girl's mom, but that shit won't last too much longer. Now sit cho ass down and don't say shit," he scolded. She sat down and surprisingly; her ass didn't say shit for real.

Heading back inside the building, I took a seat and started signing paperwork. I didn't give a fuck about what the papers said honestly, as long as the check cleared. Once everything was done, I tucked my check deep inside of my bag and headed back out the door.

When I walked out the door, Bell's brother Monte' was getting dropped off. I'm guess Bell called him to drive his car back home. Mama had no business in his shit anyway.

"Aight bruh, I'ma fuck wit cha." Dapping Bell up, he pulled off and his girl followed him out of the parking lot. Mama was sitting there looking like a bad ass kid with a whole attitude.

Bending down next to her, I looked her right in her eyes so we could have a mature conversation.

"Mama, I mean this from the bottom of my heart and I

don't want you to take this lightly at all. You need to grab whatever you have at the house, and get the hell out. I mean that in all seriousness too. Since you brought yo ass back here, you've tried to kidnap my daughter for money, stole money from Bell, stole his car, now yo ass up here trying to steal more money. What is the problem?" I really needed to know what was going through her head.

"I'm broke baby, I ain't got no money," she replied quickly trying to sound like Mitch from Paid in Full.

"So, you're having money issues?"

"Money issues, rent issues, and my health is fucking with my mental," she replied.

"A lot more gone be fucking with your mental if you keep stealing from me," Bell mumbled.

"I'm sorry for all of that but just give me one more chance to be in you guys life, the right way. My grand baby deserves to have her grandma around for more than a few days."

"How do I know that we can even trust you alone anymore? You're like a big ass kids, as soon as an adult walk away, you start doing shit that you don't have any business doing."

"You know what; she can stay, but she has to stay somewhere else and I have the perfect place for her. She gone learn to keep her hands to herself over there. Follow me." Bell announced anxiously, almost as if he was happy about the place he was taking her to. Mama looked worried but she stayed in the car with Bell, while my baby girl and I followed behind him. It took me a little minute to realize where he was going because I've only been to Cashmere's house twice. Bell got out and mama immediately locked the doors back.

I watched as he went inside and came back out with Cash who seemed to be wearing a goofy grin. Getting out, I walked toward them after telling Sunny to stay in the car.

"You know this gone cost you some more racks, right? Especially since my house is not a fucking nursing home which is obviously where her old feline ass needs to be," Cash told him making Bell and I look puzzled.

"You mean senile?" I corrected.

"No! I meant what I said. A feline is a cat, a cat is a cougar. Don't she look like one of them old ass cougars who would give up her whole check to some young nigga and take her teeth out to suck his dick?"

"Oh Lord!" We laughed at her crazy ass, as we stood back and watched her make mama open the door.

"Now you know what they like to do to old people in nursing homes. Keep playing in this man car, and you gone miss dinner and get yo ass smacked later on for not listening.

Anymore back talk, I'm dropping yo ass off at 2829 Sycamore Street. Now get out of the car and let's go." She pulled mama by her legs so hard that she slipped out of the car and bumped her head. Cash dragged her back up to the house kicking and screaming. When they made it inside the house, we walked away.

"Help! Please don't leave me here. This bitch is crazy." Before mama could get out the house, she was pulled right back in.

"Let's go because I'm not trying to be a witness to whatever she about to do to her. Call up Sasha and see where she at. She ain't say nothing about looking at the houses today or not. I guess she took the money and did what she had to do with it and don't want my help anymore."

Pulling my phone out, I called up Sasha like Bell asked, to see what she wanted to do.

"Hey boo!" I exclaimed.

"Hey Snow."

"Are you still going to look at one of Bell's places or did you change your mind?" I asked.

"I'm actually just getting back to the hotel from buying a car. I had plans to stay in one of his places, but maybe I can just go find something on my own. I don't want him thinking I'm using him, since I have money now."

"He wouldn't think that," I objected.

"How would you know, Snow?" She snapped back quickly.

"Because he is the reason why I called to see what your plans were. Even though you have money, I would still take the help from him because that allows you to have more money to put up for a rainy day and still get you and the girls a little something."

"I guess you're right. Just tell me where you want to meet up at and I'll be there." After giving her the address, we went back to the house, to drop off one of the cars so we could ride together. Once we got that done, we headed over to the condo he had downtown.

We pulled up at the same time as Sasha and the girls. They jumped out and ran over to me.

"Good morning Ms. Snow and Mr. Bell." After giving us a hug, they ran right over to Sunny. She was so caught up in the iPad that Bell bought her for Christmas that she barely looked up.

"Damn girl, that's a nice ass ride," I blurted out as I admired the Porsche truck, she pulled up in. When she said she just came from the car lot, I had no idea she meant this type of car. I know this took a nice chunk of her money.

"Thank you, the girls picked it out. They claimed they wanted to ride in style," she beamed with pride.

"Yea, but I could have saved you a lot of money. I got one of them in the garage already. I told you that I would give you a car and a place to stay. I wasn't going back on my word just because you got a hunnid grand.

Especially since, that shit won't last long unless you're

steady adding to it.

If you are spending like this, it will be gone in a

few weeks' tops. Be smart shorty." I knew what Bell

meant but judging by the way Sasha's lip turned up,

she's about to take that shit the wrong way.

"Well I'm sorry my little hunnid grand is like

fifty dollars to you. I did what I thought was right for me

and my kids. It's cold as hell and I wasn't about to keep

calling your dog headed ass brother," Sasha spat back.

"Ok now!" I interrupted, "He was only trying to

help you save money, boo. It's your money and you can

most definitely do what you want with it. Just let us

know if you want to go up to see the condo or you rather

find something on your own. It's totally up to you."

"It's cool. We can look at it," she shrugged her shoulders and walked behind Bell into the building. Once we got inside, I damn near wanted to tell him that I wanted to move in here. It was only 2 bedrooms, but extremely spacious. The floor plan was open from the kitchen, to the living room. Both of the bedrooms had bathrooms in them and there was a half bathroom in the hallway for the guest.

"Mommy, it's so nice. Can we stay here please?" the girls begged.

"You sure you don't want to look at anything else?"

"No, we want this one," they squealed.

"It's all yours then girls." Bell told them before tossing Sasha the keys. "Everything is on me for two years. The only thing you need to do today is, get some groceries cause the fridge is as naked as I'm trying to have Snow later on."

"Oh gosh," I let out.

"Thank you, Bell."

"No problem. Snow, I need to get back to the diner. You riding with me?"

"Mommy can we stay for a little while please?" Sunny asked as she ran from the back with the girls.

"I'll take you guys home later. I don't mind." Sasha told me. When I agreed to stay a little while longer, the girls ran back down the hall to play. Bell left out the door and that left Sasha and I standing here looking at each other crazy. Trying to think of something to break the ice, I asked, "So how was his sex?"

"Bittttch, it was bomb as fuck!" She blurted out anxiously like she was just waiting on me to ask that question. "It happened so fast and we probably shouldn't have done it so quickly but I don't regret it. The only thing I do regret is his ass talking to some bitch while I was shopping for the girls. He was talking about us like we weren't shit to him. I mean, we aren't but shit he is the one who asked to take us to the store then wanted to act like he was driving Mrs. Daisy around or something."

"Overall, Tim is a good guy though. I'm sure what he said wasn't all that bad."

"Poor, Snow! Even after all that you have been through, you still seem to see only the good in people. News flash; stop that shit. That's the quickest way to get your feelings hurt again. Yea Bell is a great guy, but that nigga is not flawless." To snap, or keep it cute; that is the question. Nah, fuck that.

"Let's be clear! I've never said that Bell was flawless, but until he gives me a reason to think or say those words then in my eyes, he is perfect. I don't need you to try to put anything different in my head and if you have so much negative shit to say about him, then you can give me the keys back to this condo. I mean, I wouldn't want help from someone who I think is a piece of shit."

"I never said those words," she hissed'

"You might as well have said them. What was your purpose of saying he wasn't flawless, if we were talking about you fucking his brother? Bell had nothing to do with that conversation. All I said was Tim is a great guy, and nothing is wrong with you hearing him out if he tried to contact you. Granted you guys just met, but if he was willing to do whatever he did for you then that shows he has a good heart because he didn't have to do shit."

She had really pissed me off talking about Bell when he ain't have shit to do with shit. It's not our fault she fucked Tim and now she's feeling a way about his ass. That shit is between them. Bell has been nothing but good to her since he found out who she was. At the end of the day, the nigga is trying to make shit right and I'm not about to let her or no one else, take that from him.

"I was just saying-"

"Me too!" I spoke up, cutting her off. "I was just saying if you have a problem with Bell then give me Bell's keys and you do what you have to do for you and yours from here on out."

"I'm sorry, damn! I'll take back what I said." Smirking my lips in a whatever the fuck you say manner,

I walked over and took a seat at the island. "You forgive me?"

"We cool, just watch what you say about him when the nigga has offered you everything but his first born child, to make sure you and the girls were straight."

"You're right." She walked over to me with her arms held out for a hug. I playfully rolled my eyes and held mine out too. We embraced for a moment before moving on like the conversation never happened. A little while later, we gathered the girls and headed out the door to get groceries and a much-needed bottle of wine.

On the drive to the store, I decided to text Cash to make sure she haven't killed my mama.

Me: Y'all good?

Crazy Cash: Yep, she sitting over her in this adult highchair I made her ass so she wouldn't try to run off. I got her ass strapped to the seat with a log chain. Her ass ain't going nowhere anytime soon.

Me: Ok just be careful. You don't want her to have a real heart attack this time.

Crazy Cash: You don't want her ass to be buried in my back yard either.

Me: Bye Cash

Crazy Cash: Toodles sis. I have to go anyway; Casino is on his way over here.

Me: Casino?

Crazy Cash: MYBB

Me: MYBB?

Crazy Cash: Mind Yo Business, Bitch

Me: Good fucking bye lol

Dropping my phone back in my purse, I sat back and looked out the window while I tuned out the sounds of the kids scream in my ear.

CHAPTER 10- BELL

It's the night before the New year and I got everything set up for the party that Snow wanted to plan at the last minute. She hasn't lifted a finger but she had a nigga running around like a dry hard dick with no pussy juice on it; just all fucked up. Her mama been begging to help out but Cash got her ass locked in a chamber until she learns how to respect other people property. Cash don't even know how to do that, so I found it funny that she's trying to teach someone else.

"Bruh, how many of these you got? I'm fucking tired," Monte complained as he walked inside of the building with another bouquet of long-stemmed roses. They were inside this diamond studded vase, so I'm sure they were heavy as hell. I wouldn't know for sure, because I haven't tried to pick one up.

I had something special planned for Snow and I wasn't about to wait another minute getting it done. On Christmas, I asked her to be my girl, at midnight tonight, I'm asking her to be my wife. I don't see any other woman in this world that I'd rather go through all of this shit with.

Her mama alone, would have ran a regular ass muthafucka away. But me, I'm too solid of a man to let something like that take her away from me.

"Hello nigga, how many roses does it take to show a bitch that you love her?"

"How about you buy me some for your bitch and see," I spat back.

"Stop asking him so many questions, just get the damn flowers so I can go. You promised me that you would buy me a dress for tonight and I'm not about to let

Bell and these damn flowers keep you occupied." His girl Tessa came in with a straight attitude as she walked in with roses in her hands too.

"I told yo ass I was getting you a dress. You acting like I'm taking you to the Gucci store or something. I'm giving yo ass $150.00 and you can spend that shit as you please, in Rainbow."

"Shit, she'll be able to get 5 dresses and shoes to match with that," I added.

"Oh, y'all got jokes? How about I knock all of this shit over?" she hissed. "Who told yo ass people wanted to bring in the new year at an engagement party anyway? Don't you know that's the perfect time for people to be fucking up headboards and shit?" Monte' sucked his teeth and headed back outside like her ass ain't say shit. They've been together since high school and gets on each other last nerve every single day. The only thing that holds them together, is the crazy love that they have for each other.

"Bell!" Hearing my name being called, I turned around to see Sasha walking in the building with a fruit tray. She was dressed in Fendi from head to toe so I definitely had to look again to make sure that was her. Plus, the short hair that she usually rocked, was now down to her ass.

"Damn! What happened?" I asked as she got closer to me. Shorty had so much make up caked on her face that she looked more like herself from afar. Close up, she looked like Bozo.

"What you mean? You don't like the new look?" She spun around and tossed her long ass hair from side to side. "I just wanted something different to bring in the new year. I figured if I looked like money, then I would make money the whole year." Chuckling, I shook my head no.

"That's not how that works. You actually need to be doing something to bring in money. That shit not just gone fall into your lap because you look like you got money. I'm sure not spending that much on an outfit and shoes would have made it possible for you to have even more money."

"I don't get what you and Snow want me to do with the money. I struggled for years and went without a lot just to get to this moment where we don't have to live like that anymore," she sobbed. I wasn't trying to make shorty cry; I just want her to see the value of a dollar and she not getting that shit. She went out and bought everything I told her I would give her for free. That shit made no sense at all.

"I'm just trying to make sure you not only have money but keep that shit. You feel me? Why would you want to blow through that money and have nothing else to fall back on?" Placing the tray of fruit on the table, I pulled the seat out for her to sit down. "Tell me this Sasha, what type of education do you have?"

"What does that have to do with anything?" She mumbled.

"Just answer the question."

"I dropped out of high school when I was seventeen years old," she admitted.

"Did you go back to get your G.E.D?"

"No."

"What is your plan if you actually blow through this money faster than you expected? You got a place to stay rent and utility free for two years, but what about food? Clothes for your girls, money for the little things that you guys would need. Who's going to pay for that when your money is gone?"

"You not?" She asked in all seriousness.

"Hell nah, you ain't my girl!" I replied before I knew it. "Sasha you have to think for the future. You need to go back and get your G.E.D. and if college is what you want to do, then do that shit. You have to have something going for yourself for someone to even think about hiring you for anything. What's something you always wanted to do?" I quizzed.

"I love to cook. I just never had a kitchen to do that shit in. When I stayed with my aunt, she taught me a lot on her good days and I fell in love with cooking. So, I've always thought about opening my own restaurant."

"And you can do that shit too, but you have to give these people something before they even give you a chance to do that. They just don't hand out help to people who they don't even see is trying to help themselves. Go to school, get that business degree so you can learn how to run that shit yourself.

Now that is something that I wouldn't mind investing in, but you gotta show me that's something you want. That's not something that I'm doing because of what happened to your mother either. I want to help you because I know you have the potential to be great at that shit. Probably even better than me," she laughed.

"I get it. Thank you, for everything."

"It's cool. Just don't have me wasting my money and that food nasty as hell. Matter fact, you're cooking Sunday dinner in your new place to show me you know what you're doing," I joked.

"Cool, just don't invite Tim"

"Don't invite me to what?" Tim walked in with the single cupcake that I asked him to have Snow's ring put into. "Come get this cupcake, I almost forget a ring was inside and ate this shit," he fussed as he sat the cupcake on the table. "Now, what y'all in here talking about? Don't invite me to what?"

"It was nice talking to you Bell and I promise I won't let you down." She got up from the table without acknowledging Tim. I don't know what was going on but she looked through that nigga like his mama and daddy were made of glass.

Once she walked past him, he turned and followed her out the door. As bad as I wanted to see what they had going on, I stayed inside so that I could finish getting this stuff together. About an hour later, I left out and headed to the diner to make sure they had the food ready. After this, my ass was going home to lay the fuck down. A nigga dick needs to get rubbed on before tonight and depending on how good she rocks my shit, will determine if she get that big ass eight carot oval pink diamond ring tonight.

Parking in front of the diner, I got out in a hurry once I saw the car that was parked in front of it. Seeing YO-YO on the tag, I knew Yolanda was inside and probably about to start some shit that I didn't have time for.

"You got company, boss man." Ashley pointed to my office with an unpleasant smile on her face. "You already know she with the shit so just let me know if you need me to beat her ass for you." Laughing, I kept walking towards my office. Once I walked in, she was sitting at my desk with her feet propped up.

"What's up?" I asked as I placed my coat over one of the chairs.

"We need to talk." She sat up in the chair and stared at me before speaking. "I came by here to tell you something before I officially broke things off with Prince." She got up from the desk and sashayed over towards me. Everything she had on, was tighter than a bitch head with a fresh sew in.

My eyes roamed her body but quickly snapped back up to her face. "I just thought that you should be the first to know that I'm pregnant." I stepped back, as she stepped closer to me. Sliding her hands around me, I pulled them right back off.

"The fuck does that have to do with me?" I moved around the room and everywhere I went, she followed closely behind me.

"Because it's yours! I'm eight weeks and you and I both know that you were the only dick deep inside of me at that time," she hissed.

"Shorty, if you're fucking my little brother now, then I'm sure you were fucking with more than me eight weeks ago. No disrespect, but your pussy ain't that credible no more. Plus, who's to say you weren't fucking Prince back then too?"

"Because we haven't fucked at all yet. Which is why I can't even trick him like this is his baby because he would instantly know that I was lying to him. The only thing that I can do is be honest with you, so you can stop this little charade you have going on with the Snowball chick. You know you miss me and I'm sure she's not fucking you how I used to fuck you. I used to get down and dirty with that dick, which is what you loved about me the most."

"Correction, that's what I liked about you, but my shorty be draining the shit out my dick now. So, you can go head on with that shit. Snow and I are doing great and from what I heard, so are you and my brother." Pushing her back off me, I went towards the door so that I could open it and push her ass out.

"Don't try to fight it Bell; you know you miss this," She grabbed me by my sweats and forced her hand into my boxers.

"Fuck! Stop!" I pushed that hoe so hard that she fumbled back into my desk.

"I came by to get my brother's blessing because I thought I wanted to marry you. Since he fucked you first, I wanted to make sure everything was cool with him." Once she heard Prince's voice, she stopped in her tracks. "Now that I see you ain't over him yet, I guess I'll change my plans and go find me a loyal bitch. Tim told me you weren't shit but I wanted to have faith in you."

"You wanted to marry me?" Apparently, that was the only part she heard and not the fact that he just called her ass an unloyal ass bitch.

"I wanted to! I figured I was getting older and you were the best piece of pussy that I had in a long time. That shit over with now though." He turned away and walked outside and she went running out right behind him. I was just glad her ass left out of here. What they come up with is on them, I wasn't trying to cloud my mind with no one else bullshit.

Picking up my phone, I called up Snow to tell her what just happened. Most nigga's would have kept that shit to themselves but not me. I didn't give a fuck because Yolanda wasn't shit to me anymore.

"Pregnant?" Snow screamed out.

"That's what she said but you already know she was on some more shit. Soon as Prince popped up talking about, he was about to ask her to marry him, she flew her ass out the door behind him. I already knew she would come back with something sooner or later because she walked away from me, too easily."

"Well as long as she knows that whatever you guys had before me, is over now," she paused for a second as if she were waiting on me to reply. "It is over, right Bell?"

"No doubt! You don't have anything to worry about. You just make sure you are out getting sexy as fuck for tonight."

"I don't see what I have to get this dolled up for. It's just a simple ass party with family and friends. The only family I would've had there was my mom but Cash said she's not ready to make her new appearance yet, whatever that meant."

"My family is your family," I told her trying to make her feel a little better. I had to make sure I swung by Cash's crib to make sure she let Snow's mom out for a little while.

"Yea I know and I love all of them because they really treat me like I'm a part of them."

"You're a part of me, well you will be. Once I ask you to marry me next Christmas." I paused for a second to see what she was going to say.

"Next Chrissstmas?" she dragged. "You mean to tell me that I've been putting this pussy on you only so yo ass could wait eleven more months to ask me to marry you. Ah damn! Let me leave out of this place I'm in because you don't even deserve this right now."

"Wait, where are you?" I probed.

"I was about to get my coochie waxed but since this won't be a special occasion, then I'll wait till next month. Yo ass only getting pussy once a month from now on and you better hope that day doesn't fall on a day that my cycle on."

"Shiid, a nigga be stomping through mud; you should know I don't give a fuck about fucking through blood." I told her ass the truth because I didn't give a fuck.

"Eww, nasty!" she squealed.

"Only with you. I'm about to get out of here though before Yolanda ass pop back up on some more bullshit. I'll be home in a few; I need to go by Cash's house first."

"Ok baby, I love you."

"I love yo ass too, Snow." Ending the call, I put my coat on and headed out the door. It was snowing harder than a bitch outside, and I couldn't wait to get back home. Pulling off, I headed straight to Cash's spot. When I pulled up, the place was dark as hell but her car was outside.

I knocked on the door several times, and just before I got ready to get back in my truck, some big ass nigga with a gold grill answered the door.

"Ayo, who the fuck is you and why the fuck are you coming over my girl crib?" I looked around to see who the fuck this nigga was talking to. "Nigga I'm talking to you! What the fuck you want?"

"Cash, you better come get yo boy before he loses his only life he got to live," I told her calmly as I stood there with my gun just ready to blow his fucking head off. Just cause a nigga don't look and act, street, doesn't mean that shit doesn't still run through me.

"Casino, what I tell you about answering my damn door anyway. My brother should have shot yo ass!" Cash exclaimed.

"Nah, that nigga should have announced himself before walking up the steps."

"Bruh, how the fuck was I supposed to do that shit? You know what, don't even worry about it. Where is Snow's mama?" I asked Cash, as I pushed through the door.

"She's in the kitchen in her highchair." Shaking my head, I walked away and headed into the kitchen. When my eyes landed on Ms. Daye, she looked scared and was in a complete daze. She was strapped to a chair with a tray in front of it, looking like a big ass high chair for real.

"You straight?" I asked making her jump.

"Yes, yes suh masta. I guess I can say that I am. Ms. Cashmere is treating me nicely, I even got to eat at the table today." My eyebrows snapped together quickly when I heard her ass sounding like she was a slave.

"Where do you normally eat?" I asked.

"In the basement next to her dead dog that she made me stuff. She said you killed him but she wasn't ready to let him go yet," she spoke so softly and kept looking around as if she was checking to see if Cash was coming. "Bell, I know I fucked up but please get me out of here. This bitch is crazy as fuck and I'm afraid if I don't leave soon, I just may kill myself."

"Nah, I'm not letting you do that." Getting her out of the chair, she headed right to the back to find some clothes to put on. Cash had her ass on some fucking big ass old folks diapers. "Yo Cash, I'm taking her back with me. You over her doing some weird ass shit and I don't even want her being a part of this shit."

Pausing, I looked around but didn't see Cash or her crazy ass boyfriend, Casino. "Cash!" I called out again but this time I heard loud moans coming from the bathroom.

Ms. Daye was coming from the back just in time for us to get out of here. I had to make a mental note to get my lil sister checked out. I swear since mama died, she ain't been right in the head at all.

Leaving out the house, we got inside the car and pulled off. "Thank you for that. I want you to hear me when I say this and take in every word. Your sister has some mental issues going on and she is very unstable. All her and that Casino guy do is fight and fuck.

It's crazy because you can see the love that they have for each other but they both are toxic as fuck. Help her, before that love turns into something neither one of them can control and they end up really hurting each other. I ain't never seen a bitch stab a dude then go stitch him back up herself. That's some unstable as shit."

"I'll talk to her. I noticed her change but thought she would get over it and it was just a phase after losing our mom. Seems like this shit is lasting a little too long and I can't let my sister go out like that. I'll make sure she is straight, even if it's the last thing I do."

Stopping at the light, I turned my windshield wipers up higher so that I could clear out all of the snow that was coming down fast.

"BELL, LOOK OUT!" Ms. Daye screamed out while beating on my arm and pointing towards the bus that was speeding right towards up. Before I could react, the bus ran into the driver side of my truck and flipped us over four times. As soon as the truck stopped flipping, the back end caught on fire.

We landed on the roof of the truck and there was no way I could get us out of here because it was crushed enough to trap us in. Ms. Daye was going in and out of consciousness and no matter what I said to her, she wouldn't stay up. "Just hold on, I got you." I told her as I started yelling out of help.

"Just stay calm, I've already called for help," Looking up into a stranger's eyes, I nodded my head because at this time, the smoke was making me feel dizzy. "Help me! This truck is going to blow." He yelled out to someone.

I couldn't do anything but pray and asked God to have mercy on my soul. I prayed this was not my karma for what happened to Sasha's mom. Whatever it was, I couldn't do anything but hope God saw us through it. I held on to Ms. Daye's hand before I heard a loud

explosion, and everything turned black.

CHAPTER 11- SNOW

I arrived at the party and to my surprise, Bell ass was nowhere to be found. We had already made plans to arrive separately but now I wished he had come with me. Everybody was here with their dates and I was sitting in the corner looking like a lonely fool. I tried calling his phone several times, but all of my calls went unanswered. Walking around, I tried to look as unbothered as I possibly could, but I couldn't.

I found myself checking outside every two minutes to see if he was pulling up. Picking up my phone again, only to reach his voicemail. "What the fuck is taking you so long? I swear to fucking gawd, if you are out there fucking off with that Yolanda bitch then I promise you, we are done." Ending the call, I hung up and called right back. "Baby, for real, where are you?" I whined into the receiver.

"You heard from Bell yet?" Monte' walked up on me and asked. Shaking my head, no, he walked off after telling me that he was going to call him. I turned away from the window once I saw Cash and her guy pull up. When I didn't see my mama with her, I rushed outside to see why she didn't bring her to the party with her.

"Cash, where is my mama?" Shrugging her shoulders, she walked past me, but I pulled her right back. "What do you mean, you don't know? We left her with you and now you don't know where she is?"

"Right, and apparently she was in better hands with me because Bell came and got her a few hours ago and now you don't know where she is. Call him and see where they are, cause if you pull me like that again, I'ma forget you sis. Aight?" I huffed loudly in frustration as she walked away from me. Worry started to really set in, and I was about to lose my mind. *Ok, Snow, just calm down. They are all good and will be pulling up any moment now.*

"Hey boo, come over here with me." Sasha called out to me. Placing my cup down, I dragged myself over there hoping she could ease my worried mind.

"Give me some of that," I told her as I pointed to the White Hennessey behind her.

"What do you want it mixed with?"

"Nothing just give me the bottle. I'm so stressed out right now. I haven't heard from Bell or Mama and it's going on twelve o'clock. I just know something bad has happened; I can feel it in my heart." I chugged the Hennessey until it was snatched away from me. "What the fuck?" I spat, "Why would you do that?" I asked

Tim.

"You gone make yourself sick drinking that shit

like that."

"Did I ask you to worry about me? No! So just

leave me alone and let me do what I want to do. I'm a

grown ass woman and the only person who has a say so

over what I do, is your brother and I don't see his bitch

ass around here anywhere. He probably out with that

bitch, Yolanda. She popped up at his diner earlier today

talking about she's pregnant and shit. He probably got

my mama sitting in the car while he's with her."

"Just calm down! Once my brother is done

fucking with a bitch, he's done. So, don't even speak on

him like that again. If that nigga ain't here, it's a damn

good reason and Yolanda definitely is not one of the

reasons. You need to be calling around to see if that nigga straight, instead of accusing him of shit," he told me.

"That's your brother, you get yo dog as away from here and find out where he is. She is already stressed out and don't need you coming over with that shit," Sasha snapped back on him.

"Whoa shorty, who you calling a dog? I ain't did shit to you and we already talked about this shit earlier. Don't bring up old shit. I told you ain't shit happen with me and that girl. We just caught up and that was it. We didn't even fuck, as bad as I wanted to. The only thing I kept thinking about was how your homeless pussy had my ass stuck already.

You and I ain't shit right now but cool anyway. Once we talk about being more than friends, that's when you have a right to get mad, until then just fuck me and leave everything else alone. Now go get the girls so we can find my brother." Sasha ain't say shit back to Tim. She just got up like that nigga said and went to get the girls. He must have really put that dick on her cause ain't no way a nigga gone call my pussy homeless and still expect me to ride with him. Ion care if I was homeless or not. She should have smacked his ass for that shit, then went and got the girls like he said.

"Yall gone be ok riding together?" I asked Tim.

"Yea, she'll be ok later on tonight. She ain't had none in a few days. Good dick make you lash out like that."

"Lord, you and your brother are both crazy cause he seems to think the same shit." Laughing, I took the bottle back out of his hand and poured me a cup and mixed it with some shit that Sasha had on the table. "My

bad for snapping on you like that."

"It's cool, we're all good." He walked off and

headed over to where Monte' and Prince were standing.

The only thing I could do was continuously call Bells

phone and pray he walked through that door soon.

"Hello!" Pausing, I pulled the phone back from

my ear when I heard another females voice on the other

end of Bells phone.

"Um, who is this and where is Bell?" I quizzed.

"I'm nurse Coleman. Are you a close relative of

Bell?"

"Why, what's wrong?" I replied quickly.

"Something happened and I just need to get in

touch with a close relative."

"Bitch, if you don't tell me what the fuck is going on, I swear!" I let out and by this time Sasha was standing beside me looking crazy, while trying to see what was going on. "I am as close of kin as you are about to get, so tell me what's going on. I've been looking for him for hours and calling his phone like crazy. Now tell me where he is so I can come pick him up."

"I'm sorry, there's been a terrible accident. Bell was in a car accident with a Mona Daye, the car exploded and-" Dropping the phone, I let out a loud cry as I dropped down to my knees. Sasha picked up the phone, but I was crying so loud that I couldn't hear what she was saying.

Feeling my body being lifted, I was carried to the back of someone's SUV before everyone else jumped in.

The truck took off fast as hell and the only thing that was going through my head was how I lost Bell before I even had a chance to love him properly.

A little while later, we pulled up to the hospital and got out. I dragged my feet because identifying his body was nothing that I wanted to take part in. "Come on Snow," Sasha shouted at me, snapping me out of the daze that I was in.

"What's the rush? He's dead!" Shrugging my shoulders, I turned around and headed back to the truck when those words left my mouth.

"Dead? Bell is not dead. He was in a bad wreck with your mom, but no one died. She did say that he got burned really bad   before the bystanders were able to pull them out of the car."

"What? He's not dead?" Bigger tears filled my eyes, as I ran inside just in time to catch his brothers and sisters, getting on the elevator. I waited anxiously for the doors to open and once they did, I ran out like a bat out of hell down the hall towards, ICU.

"Which way is Bell Whyte's room?" I frantically asked. "Wait, my mom! Where is Mona Daye's room?"

She pecked on the computer before telling me that Bell requested them to be in the same room. Rushing down the hall, I ran into the room and almost died when I saw Bell laying there. He had bandages around his head and only had a space open for his mouth and eyes. His legs were propped up in a cast as if they were broken and one of his arms were wrapped up as well. I walked over to him slowly and stood next to his bed.

"Bell," I whispered and hoped like hell that he could hear me. "Bell baby, it's me, Snow." He groaned before squeezing my hand.

"I'm sorry, baby! This is not how I wanted to bring in the New Year."

"Shh, it's ok. You just get some rest and we will worry about everything else later," I told him as I pulled a chair up beside his bed.

"Umm, yo mama is over here too!" *Oh Shit.* Jumping up, I walked over to her side of the room to make sure she was ok. She had a few bruises and burns but nothing compared to Bell. I'm just glad they both were still alive.

"You ok ma?" I asked.

"Yea baby, I'm fine. Your man is not though. I saw him before they wrapped him up and he look like that actor Seal, but ten times worse," She whispered to me so that Bell couldn't hear her. Looking back over at Bell, I smiled because no matter what he looked like underneath; I'm going to love him anyway. He found a way to love me through the rough place that I was in and there's no way I wouldn't do the same for him.

"I'll be right back ma." I got up from the chair that was beside her bed and walked back over to Bell. Grabbing his hand, I kissed the back of it before sitting wherever I could on the bed with him.

"Snow."

"Yes, Bell! I'm right here." I blurted out quickly.

"I know a nigga doped on all types of medicines and shit so I can't feel the pain, but I still have something I wanted to ask you. I'm not about to let this or anything else get in my way. First, I need you to call a doctor in here." Doing as he asked, I got up and headed out the door. His family all poured in, as I left out the room. Grabbing one of the doctors, we headed back into the room.

His family were all crowded around him grinning like this wasn't a sad ass occasion. Ignoring them, we walked around the other side of his bed. "How may I help you, Mr. Bell?"

"I need you to unwrap my face," Bell requested.

"Are you sure that's what you want me to do? I think it's best that we leave the bandages on right now and just get some rest." The doctor insisted.

"No, I want you to take them off."

"How about we-" before he could object again, Cashmere, Monte', Prince and Tim all had guns at his head. "How about bout I call one of the nurses to get these bandages removed for you as soon as possible. Will there be anything else?" His attitude changed to Benson really quick.

"No, thank you." Nodding his head, he quickly hustled out of the room.

"How yall asses get those guns in the hospital?" Sasha probed.

"It doesn't matter. My brother about to pay a high as medical bill to that muthafucka and if he asks for anything then they need to be on that shit; pronto." Monte' replied.

The nurse came rushing into the room and started easing the bandages off Bell's face carefully. The more she unwrapped, the more everyone's face turned away in the room. Except mine, I wanted to see exactly what he looked like now so that I could fall in love with him all over again.

"Oh, my damn! Wrap him back up." Cash blurted out before pretending to gag.

"You're so fucking rude. Take yo ass out in the hallway. This is your brother and he could have been dead and the only thing you see are the scars. Grow the fuck up, Cash." Everyone looked at Cash then back at her boyfriend, who I found out name was Casino. Weird but hey, they are crazy and cute together.

"Boy fuck you!" She hissed back before taking her ass out the door like he said.

"I'm sorry Bell. I'll work with her on that attitude of hers. She be doing too much at the wrong time." Casino told Bell, before leaving out of the room behind her.

"Snow, I know this doesn't look like the man you fell in love with, but I swear on the inside I'm still him. I still want to love you for the rest of my life, if you will still love me back. I may be an ugly sight to look at, but I'll be the ugliest, happiest, muthafucka on Earth as long as I get to love my girl forever. I had plans to ask you at the party, but since I missed it, I want to ask you right now.

Snow Daye, can you see pass this rough ass exterior and marry a nigga? I need you in my life and there's no one else in this world that I would want to go through this journey with. I love you and Sunshine with all of my heart," he paused for a second before reaching under his covers.

"Boy you better not pull that burnt ass dick out," Tim scolded.

"Nigga!" was all Bell said before he pulled a box from under the covers then opened it. The ring was so beautiful and but I was confused why it had what looked like icing on some parts of it. "Don't worry about the crumbs, I had intention to give this to you in a cupcake but it got smashed in the accident. So, what you say Snow, am I still good enough for you?"

"YES! YES! YES!" I squealed before jumping on the bed, only to make him cry out in pain. "Fuck, I'm so sorry baby."

"Will you marry me, right now?" he asked.

"Right now? But how? Where? Who's going to marry us?" I rambled off so many questions back to back.

"Let me handle that part." Prince left out of the room and returned a little while later with the Chaplin.

"We gotta do this shit quick. He was in the middle of praying for a family who just lost their daddy. I tapped him on the shoulder with my gun like 'cuse me. Let me holla at you for a second." We all shook our heads at Prince crazy ass.

"Go get the doctor again." This time Sasha left out and came back in.

"Is there anything else I can do for you?" He asked as he stood next to the bed.

"Yes, I need a private empty room so I can marry my girl in, right now."

"Are you sure you want this to happen right now?" I quizzed.

"I wanted to marry you next Christmas with snow all around us and everybody in all white. This is the closest I will get to that right now."

"Right now it is then. I've been Dreaming of a Whyte Wedding, since the moment I laid eyes on you," I expressed.

"Well then, let's make this shit happen because I can't wait to change your name to Mrs. Snow Whyte."

Epilogue

One year later

Bell and Snow

After several surgeries and a lot of money spent, a nigga face looked halfway normal. They thought they were about to do some face off shit on me, but I wasn't having that. Make me look like me and no one else.

Life has been amazing for me and Snow since the day we said, I do. She finally got the shelter and the orphanage running smoothly. She even found a way to get most of the kids adopted.

Cash, even stepped up and adopted her a little boy. He was only a few months old but he's one now and bad as hell. She's having his birthday party today and I started to not get the little venom teeth fucka anything because he bit the shit out of me the other day.

Pulling up to the party, Snow waited on me to get out and open the door up for her. Once I did, she slid out and wobbled her juicy ass to the door of Cash's house. She looked so beautiful pregnant and I couldn't wait to see what our little Prince and Princess were going to look like. God blessed us with twins, and I think I was more excited than Snow was.

"Cash! Where's the food?" Snow yelled out as she searched the house for food.

"Food? Didn't you read your invitation?" Cash asked, looking puzzled as hell.

"Ugh yes! You are having a party for Colston and you wanted us to by of ad. I thought that was a different type of meal or something you were making for the party."

"Bitch, that said B.Y.O.F.A.D as in, Bring Your Own Food and Drinks!"

"I know you fucking lying! Let's go Bell cause sis got me fucked up if she thought I was about to bring my own food to a damn birthday party. Hey nephew, bye nephew. I'ma curse my mama out for not telling me the shit Cash was on." Snow fussed as she wobbled right out the door just as slow as her ass wobbled in.

Cash and Ms. Daye became close friends and now you can't keep them two apart. She's Colston God grandmother and they stay attached at the hip too.

I gave lil man his gift before following behind Snow out the door. "Your sister needs help, Bell."

"I know baby. Let's just get y'all fed first because you know if your juicy ass doesn't eat every three hours, you'll have a bitch fit." She started dancing in her seat while rubbing her stomach.

"You damn right." Leaning over, I kissed her on the lips before focusing back in the road. I prayed that things kept going great for us as we continued to grow in love, God and complete our beautiful family.

Sasha and Tim

Life was good. I don't even know how much I could stress that shit. I've never been so happy and complete in my life. I went back to school as Bell suggested to get my G.E.D. I passed with flying colors and enrolled into some business classes. Next step, we are definitely opening up this restaurant. My girls have been enjoying being kids and doing what the other kids do without feeling left out.

Chuck E' Cheese is now a small place to them and they ask Tim to take them to Dave and Buster's. They are growing up to be perfect pretty little women and I can't ask for anything better.

"Baby, why you gotta take all day to get ready? You know Cash gone cut up if we are late for this lil bad ass boy party." Turning around, I smile at my man before cursing his ass out.

"Boy fuck Cash. Snow already texted me and told me the girl wanted us to bring the food and the drinks to a party she's having for her own child. Who does that? She knows damn well, that's not how a party works." He laughed, then shook his head.

"So, I guess Snow left to get herself some food?"

"You already know, and we are about to meet her at the restaurant. I'll drop Colston his gift off but I'm not about to attend a foodless party. Now come help me put these shoes on."

"You might want to start with getting a matching pair. You can't see over that big ass stomach?" Tim joked and I didn't find that shit funny at all. Yesterday, I turned six months and I couldn't wait to get this big-headed ass boy out of me. For Tim to talk so much shit

about my homeless pussy, he sure didn't waste any time

knocking my ass up and making me his girl.

Over the past year, we have grown so much

closer. Before we started dating, he became my best

friend and he went to every single counseling session

with me. That really helped us out even more. It showed

that he really wanted to be there for me and was trying to

get me back to my fullest potential. I lacked a lot because

I was holding on to so much anger that stopped me from

moving on and growing more; mentally and spiritually.

I slipped up a lot and started blowing money and

if it wasn't for him and Bell getting me on the right

track, our asses would have been on the streets again. I

thank God for this family coming into my life and giving

me a family again. Everything was unexpected but came

at the most perfect time. I must admit, I loved it here.

The End

Made in the USA
Coppell, TX
17 November 2021

65934244R00134